Guano donates either some or all earnings from the sale of this book—depending on how pissy he's feeling—to the United Nations Population Fund. The UNFPA provides women's reproductive health services and promotes the rights of women around the world.

AMERICAN GUANO

AMERICAN GUANO

OR

ANAL PEARLS BEFORE SWINE

Give Whitey Five Press

We believe in the free and reciprocal exchange of information for educational and revolutionary endeavors.
Contact us at guano@givewhiteyfive.com for information and use.

"Agent Orange Victims" photo obtained courtesy of AlexisDuclos.com via Wikipedia.org

Published by Give Whitey Five Press
www.givewhiteyfive.com

Cover courtesy of Rotkilt Industries, Inc.

Book design by Chinook Design, Inc.
www.chinooktype.com

ISBN: 978-0-9786286-3-5

First Edition 2011

If human beings were shown what they're really like, they'd either kill one another as vermin, or hang themselves.

—Aldous Huxley

Don't blame me, I'm just holding up the mirror.

—Guano

So I'm humping the leg of Texas Justice.

Jealous?

His Christian name is Buck—Buck Masters. But when you're intimate with someone special, you call them Texas Justice.

My Christian name is Guano. My literary agent says the best way to whore myself out to some supranational book publishing corporation is to write a kiss-and-tell steaming pile about whores and priests and celebrities and individuals with the veneer of interestingness because you're so not individual or interesting and conspiracies and Knights Templar conspiracies and all other things anilingus. Modern reading dullards (repetitive) scarf it up like dogs scarfing up their own feces which modern reading dullards enjoy reading about in order to vicariously experience dog feces by way of interestingly veneered individuals and dogs peddling literary dog shit through the imperious corporate mass media's supranational book publishing corporations.

Texas Justice is a thousand feet off the ground and free-falling. I'm at his side, humping. He pops a parachute. I pop a red rocket. *New York Times* Bestseller List, here I cum! Ha!

We land on the prison rooftop. Yay! Awesome job! There to greet us (*thwap!* the sound of awesome fist punching face):

- Lucky Lonestar, code name: Lonestar

- Red Hardtongue, code name: Hardtongue
- Hoss Bullchatter, code name: Cock 'n Bull
- Thick Bullard, code name: Brooding Sartrean Existentialism

"We are the brain and backbone of an elite American commando team," says the team in unison while slapping each other's asses. "At least the backbone, anyway. There is no brain, obviously, except for maybe Hymie Hymenberg, code name: CPA. When fellow Americans find trouble in uncooperative foreign states, they call us."

The team had been recruited into service together (Jew not included). It was one of those sweltering Texas afternoons. Bodily fluids dripped from every orifice. The strapping young lads were down on the border horsin' around, hog-tying some illegals. Then they were called to an equally high cause. Behind a bush was the top-secret program's head honcho, code name: Burning Bush. After letting the gang get the gang-raping/setting afire of the Mexicans out of their system, the bush invited the boys in squirrelly Texas drawl to "Continue to defend the Fatherland by perfecting your God-given talents of incinerating foreigners." The boys thanked the bush for the compliment and were whisked to a classified military training camp where they would soon become the most murderous heroes on the planet.

Here they were teamed with (*thwap!*): two darkies from the 'hood, Climaxum "Ax 'Em" Jackson and younger soul brother Styrofoam Jackson; two Chicanos from the barrio, Jesus "The Savior" and Pancho "The Yard Man"; and the aforementioned Hymie from probably a bank somewhere to form the most lethal multiethnic fighting force this side of Skokie, Illinois.

These were the men who Texas Justice trusted with his life. Except for the blacks, Mexicans, and Jew.

I was thrown in because capitalism's every enterprise needs furry spectacular diversions to keep you slaves stupid, greedy, and lazy. Plus I can lick my own penis. Not even Jesus can lick his own penis. Ho ho! How dare I suggest that Jesus has a penis; and can't lick it. Let the death threats begin!

Texas Justice draws from his hip holster the nickel-finish pearl-grip 1873 Colt .45 Peacemaker, whirls around a few times, and fires without balancing or focusing. I continue to hump his leg. The bullet ricochets around the prison rooftop, through a steel door, through the heartless heart of a guard behind the door, out of the heart, down a stairwell, through a guy, and others, caroming off walls, wrists, spinal cords, a variety of organs, meats, and meat by-products, felling the eighteen guards working their way up the stairs, plus John F. Kennedy. Governor John Connally: wounded!

"Now that's what I call number one with a *magic* bullet!" zings Lucky Lonestar.

Texas Justice blows the smoke from his pistol's barrel. The team slaps and grabs each other's asses. Dozens of blood-snorting guards trample over the dead guards, up the stairwell, through the steel door, spilling onto the roof. Texas Justice whirls and pulls from his hip holster a forty-one-inch-long XM214 machine gun made by General Electric. GE: We bring good things to life.

Firing one hundred rounds per second, Texas Justice's GE's XM214 vaporizes the first guard rushing from the door. And the second. And the third. And the forty-ninth. The guards' transformation from bipedal hominids into fine mist of blood and entrails creates no unsightly stacks of bodies that can impede the continued flow of guards from stairwell into stream of ammunition. Two minutes and twelve thousand rounds later, the last evildoer dives into bullets and turns into fog. Final score: Texas Justice 329, Evildoers 0. The death count falls short of our preceding tour in Afraq'n'stan because of all the easily snipered orphanage children insurgents there. But that was war and we have to teach them freedom. To consume.

Texas Justice blows smoke from his forty-one-inch-long weapon.

"Now that's what I call a *blow job!*" zings Lucky.

The team grabs each other's crotches. I continue to hump leg.

Texas Justice whirls around and draws from his hip holster a B-61 tactical thermonuclear bomb. Out of the mist crawls a mewing kitten. Bellowing a hearty laugh, he reholsters the B-61 thermonuclear bomb, its two neutron generators supplied by General Electric. GE: We bring good things to life.

"Let's roll!" the team shouts in unison. We roll over the mewing kitten and down the stairwell. It leads to a cell-house corridor. Here the inmates celebrate the guards' demise by screaming gibberish, burning toilet paper, and violating each other's sphincters.

"Lucky bastards," Lucky sighs.

Texas Justice rushes with seventy-pound Andalusian Snatch Shepherd (purebred) humping his leg to the cells at the end of the hall. He twangs to the American prisoners there: "We've come to get ya out!"

Problemo: All the cells are locked shut. The control room that opens them is locked shut. The guard in the control room refuses to help us because he's a cloud on the roof. Texas Justice thumbs his B-61 nuke. Surprisingly he thinks better of it and drawls, "Lucky, come 'ere!"

"Yeah, Buck?"

"Get yer Aussie stick."

Lucky, an avid collector of all fine things Australian, carries with him at all times: an Aborigine's shrunken head on key-chain, a book on the revival of Aristotelianism in the sixteenth century, a "Wish you were here!" postcard showing a dingo eating a baby.

Lucky throws his boomerang showing Paul Hogan eating a baby through the iron bars of the control room, hitting a lever which opens all the prison cell doors. Nineteen prisoners jump out of their cells and are vaporized by Texas Justice. But unlike the courageous guards, the remaining non-vaporized inmates do not continue to dive into his ammunition. It seems even in this strange land, criminals are as cowardly as those back home.

The boomerang zings back to Lucky who zings: "Now that's what I call *return to sender!*"

Texas Justice calls out to the men we've come for: "You twelve boys, come on out now."

The Americans cry, "OK, but don't vaporize us." Texas Justice thumbs his B-61 nuke but surprisingly thinks better of it.

With the hostages now safe, Lucky zings his boomerang at the control-room lever. The prison doors slide shut. "I guess you could say the case against these cons is *open and shut!*"

We lead the detainees down the corridor to the stairwell. Then from behind us: *"Aaaaarughumfp!"*

"Only Barbra Streisand makes a sound that ill-natured!" I bark.

Texas Justice spins around and fires his Colt .45. The bullet ricochets down the corridor, through the prison cells and remaining inmates.

Zinger: "Now that's what I call *biting the bullet!*"

A twenty-foot-thick concrete wall explodes. Punching through is the warden: *"Aaaaarughumfp!"*

Lucky, Hoss, and Red look at each other and laugh and French kiss each other's asses and mosey to the middle of the corridor to meet the warden. "Hey, Brooding Sartrean Existentialism," addresses Texas Justice, "get yer sweet ass and the hostages' sweet asses to the roof."

"But what about you, Buck?" asks Brooding Sartrean Existentialism.

"I'm stayin' here. There's gonna be a showdown."

"I abhor violence," I bark, "only when it's directed towards me. Hence it's to the roof for this sweet ass; just to be safe."

"Quit yer bitchin'. Duty calls: keep humpin' my leg."

A sagebrush tumbles by. Lucky, Hoss, and Red vs. the warden in a good ol' Texas stare down! The warden strikes first, flexing his meat till shirt, slacks, and blazer explode away. Leaving only oiled muscle; and loincloth.

Lucky, Hoss, and Red consider. Then applaud enthusiastically.

The warden is six feet, nine inches—wide. Fourteen feet tall in a pair of wingtips. And loincloth.

The warden's head is hairless. He has long pointy ears, no eyes, a criminal nose. His mouth boasts sharp jagged teeth, a forked tongue, slobber, and big fireballs.

"Yentl," belches the warden.

"I don't have to take that from you, you pig-eyed sack of shit!" shouts Red.

"All right, boys! Let's do the *monster mash!*" zings Lucky, zinging boomerang into the warden's mouth.

The warden swallows. As you know. The boys applaud enthusiastically.

The warden thrusts his anvil fist against to-die-for washboard abs. With the power of Almighty Heimlich he regurgitates the boomerang. Traveling at the speed of light, how long will it take the boomerang to disintegrate Red Hardtongue's ribs and launch him fifty yards down the corridor into the stairwell?

A. All of the above.
B. A boomerang cannot travel the speed of light unless it's got a kick-ass rear spoiler.
C. I'm masturbating under my desk.
D. $4.04
E. So my only choices are to do well enough on your standardized testing to gain admittance into some

> university where I will be herded into a highly specialized, narrowly focused, highly myopic, probably soul-deadening profession that is directly or indirectly contributing to the environmental devastation of my home and life-support system thanks to its incorporation in a global capitalist economy based on constant expansion and therefore intrinsically unsustainable and suicidal in order to earn enough money to consume the never-ending consumables the advertising and marketing industry has brainwashed me into believing are necessary for life; or to fuck up your test and live in a trailer? Well well. An old-fashioned Columbine shooting is sounding better and better.

Red Hardtongue flies fifty yards down the corridor and crashes in the stairwell, ribs disintegrated.

"Looks like he took quite a *ribbing!*" zings Lucky.

The boomerang dislodges itself from Red's thorax and flies back to the warden. He stations it suggestively in his loincloth.

"Enough of this cock 'n bull!" Cock 'n Bull lowers his head and charges the enemy. But the warden is expert with loincloth, using it as a cape to guide Bullchatter past him. Another charge, another sidestep, another pass. "*¡Olé!*" I bark.

Enraged, Bullchatter ferociously charges at the fluttering loincloth. The warden again diverts him to the side, this time stabbing him between the shoulder blades with a big twelve inches of fingernail.

Lucky: "Now that's what I call a real *pain in the neck!*"

Cock 'n Bull plunges to the ground but is emotionally lifted when the warden swings his tree leg into him, launching him fifty yards down the corridor into the stairwell into Red Hardtongue.

Lucky: "I guess Cock 'n Bull got a real *kick* out of you! But you won't *kick* me to the curb!" Lucky kicks the warden so the warden grabs Lucky's leg and rips it off. "I guess he's got a *leg up* on the competition!" zings Lucky as he's being physically investigated with his own appendage in the manner the NYPD investigates dark-skinned immigrants with a toilet plunger. "Louima was *stuck* with a *stick* of a broom!" corrects Lucky, an expert in all things assault and sodomy. "You can't beat this with a stick!" zings Lucky as the warden swings Lucky's leg fast enough to dislodge and launch Lucky fifty yards down the corridor into the stairwell into Hardtongue 'n Cock 'n Bull.

Lucky: "That's why *swingers* like me *fly* first class!"

"Stop yer horsin' around and get to the roof!" orders Texas Justice.

Lucky: "But the warden's still got my leg!"

"Pull yourself together!" orders Texas Justice. "Now you leave the warden to me, lil' pardner."

"But he'll kill you, Buck."

The scene's sentimental piano music playing in the background pauses. "He'll kill me over my dead body," Buck assures. Music swells. They kiss. Each other's assholes.

Lonestar, Hardtongue, and Bullchatter jump to their feet or foot and run to the roof. Texas Justice whirls around a few times and fires without balancing or focusing. He empties twenty thousand rounds into the warden who is unfazed.

The warden draws from his loincloth Lucky's boomerang, Lucky's leg, and an XM214 machine gun and empties twenty thousand rounds into the head of Texas Justice!

And Buck Masters falls to the ground.

The CH-47 Chinook heavy-lift helicopter is too large to land on the prison roof so it lowers down a chain with a big cage attached which the commandos and hostages pile into. Then gunfire erupts from the four guard towers surrounding the cell house.

"We're taking a lot of heat up here!" radios down the chopper pilot.

Brooding Sartrean Existentialism grabs his walkie-talkie: "Niggers 'n spics: *fire!*" From hidden ground positions: Ax 'Em, Styrofoam, The Savior, and The Yard Man lay down a suppressing fire in the form of four bazooka shots which, along with a hefty bill from the Jew, collapse the four guard towers.

"OK then!" radios the pilot. "But I still got a mean crosswind up here! We need to scoot!"

"But ya never leave a man behind!" radios Brooding Sartrean Existentialism. "Texas Justice, you listenin' to all this? We're runnin' outta time up here! We need ya, buddy! Can ya hear me?"

Buck Masters' walkie-talkie is functioning, but he isn't. Mentally. As usual.

The warden leans over Texas Justice's lifeless remains, deeply inhaling, savoring the smell of the face that he would suck off the bone, spit into a refrigerator to keep it from spoiling, go upstairs, destroy the helicopter, come back down and put the face in a microwave for three minutes and forty-five seconds, set the table, serve and eat with a flan and peppy spritzer while ass-raping Ottoman Dinglies Retriever (purebred) who remains faithfully at Texas Justice's side. Humping.

But the warden didn't account for one thing: *Texas Justice!*

Buck Masters opens his eyes and says, "Well, hell! Ever'one in Texas knows you never shoot a man in his ten-gallon camouflaged bulletproof cowboy hat!" while reaching under the warden's loincloth and jamming his fist up the asshole's asshole.

Texas Justice, still lying prostrate, examines the warden's prostate.

If the prison boss had been a traditionalist and followed his inmates' regimen of packing one's asshole full of glass shards and other recyclables he may have been able to repel Buck's advances. But a traditionalist and Richard Gere he was not. "Looks like Buck's dug in deeper than a Texas tick!" zings Lucky.

Texas Justice rummages around looking for bargains then withdraws his arm and upper shoulder from the warden. A small audible pop heralds the end of the exam. Get it? *End* of the exam? Ha!

The warden is in the market for a coup de grâce so he grabs a club (Lucky's leg) and prepares to bludgeon Texas Justice. And Buck only smiles. Because just before the warden falls over dead, Texas Justice shows him the lubed and scented proctological rubber examination glove now grasping: *the warden's own still-beating heart!*

"Sorry, boys!" radios the Chinook pilot. "We gotta git or this wind is gonna take us down!"

"But ya never leave a man behind!" weeps Brooding Sartrean Existentialism.

"Yeah, never mind about leaving a dog behind, fucko," I bark.

Chopper and dangling cage strain upward. Chopper clears flaming guard tower. Dangling cage crashes through tower. But there's one thing they didn't account for: *Texas Justice!*

Texas Justice bursts from the stairwell and sprints across the prison roof. He runs sort of fast with a dog humping his leg. We reach the brick parapet and run through it. But that's not all!

Traveling at the speed of light, how long will it take a ginormous imbecile (clinically diagnosed) and Alangu Elongated Pointer expert in grinding genitalia in a press-and-release pattern (purebred) to launch 350 yards from prison roof into helicopter flying away at 125 miles per hour?

A. I'm masturbating under my desk.

B. $4.04

We rocket into the chain hanging under the helicopter. "Yeehaw!" Texas Justice whoops, grabbing chain with one hand while whooping and waving ten-gallon camouflaged bulletproof cowboy hat with the other.

"Yeehaw!" the gang heehaws from the cage below. "You ride it, ol' Buck! Just like you ride the steers 'n queers back home!"

And Texas Justice did ride that cage home; all the way home to the land of justice! *Texas* Justice!

One week later.

Buck Masters walks into the military hospital to visit his wounded team members. His wounded friends.

The prognosis is good for Red Hardtongue. He was out a rib, but if that didn't stop Adam from knocking up Eve it wouldn't stop Red from knocking up some more ten-year-old Mexicans.

Hoss Bullchatter is doing well. The warden's talon had not severed his spine, but had pierced his brain. Not serious, considering the patient.

Lucky Lonestar is another matter. Buck's best friend is a cripple. And now he had lost a leg too.

"We did it all for a just cause, didn't we, Buck?" cries Lucky.

"Yeah, lil' buddy. We did it just 'cause." Buck wipes the tears from Lucky's swollen eyes and orifices.

"For freedom?" cries Lucky.

"For freedom," Buck consoles, crawling into Lucky's bed.

"For the children?" wails Lucky.

"For the children." They spoon. "You'll see, lil' pardner. Before you know it you'll be hoppin' around, hoppin' on some little señorita who probably has a clubfoot so she can't outrun ya, and using that third leg ya got tucked in yer britches that delightfully dangles between yer first leg and second leg which got torn off to pump out some illegitimate children of yer own."

"Oh, who are we kidding, Buck? Those little *panochas* are quick as a cat—*pussy*cat! There ain't one slow enough I can knock down and ride."

The scene's sentimental piano music pauses. "Well," Buck smiles, "maybe this'll help." He unzips his jeans and pulls out: Lucky's boomerang!

(Magical tinkling sound.)

"The warden sends it with his warmest regards."

"Well, I'll be!" shouts Lucky. "Ain't you just full of surprises, you ol' coon dog!"

"You don't know the half of it!" grins Buck, whipping from his pants: Lucky's missing leg! Which I'm humping!

(Magical tinkling.)

"Yeehaw!" heehaws Lucky.

"I don't think the warden'll be missin' it!" roars Buck. "But he may be missin' this!": pulling from his pants the warden's still-beating heart!

"Guess that's what he gets for *not having a heart!*" zings Lucky. Magical tinkling sound.

"Doc says he can sew it on ya this afternoon! You'll be walkin' outta here and rustlin' up some Juarez whores tonight!"

Music swells.

"God bless you, Buck," chokes Lucky.

"God bless you, lil' fella."

They draw close, looking into each other's eyes; slowly, steadily, erectly giving each other: two big thumbs-up!

The governor of Oregon formally complains that it is his state's right to legislate and enforce its own laws. This includes the Oregon Legislature's recent abolishment of the state's death penalty and the subsequent commuting of the state's twelve death row inmates to life-in-prison sentences. In retort, Texas Governor Bush reasons that since his state has no death row inmates left after recently executing all 86,248 of them, and whereas not enough mud folk and white trash could be rustled up quick enough, and that his state might get rusty at killing folks from the lack of practice, which would be a real shame because Texas is real good with a needle, chair, pitchfork, whatever else you got, and that seeing as how the Oregon government had shirked its duty to uphold the original sentences of said twelve convicted felons, it was his state's right to liberate the twelve, fly them to Texas, and electrocute them until their nads exploded. The remnants of nads being sold on eBay with proceeds benefitting victims' families and abstinence-only sex ed programs.

The Texas governor further asserts that the gaping chasm between states rich and poor in death row inmates morally mandates that government intercedes to more equitably distribute death row inmates. Although he does grant this is a dangerous precedent to set for wealth-distribution reasons.

And then Governor Bush was crowned president.

A DOG CALLED GUANO

So I'm humping the leg of Texas Justice. Just another day of military life.

Then the team gets shipped back to Ihumpinstan for some massacres there. While serving one's country overseas by freeing Third World drones so they may someday become First World clones or at least part of the First World's cheap labor pool and most of all freeing Third World resources so they may be consumed by First World clones via First World corporations, sometimes you have to break a few eggs to make an American Imperial Omelette. And the egg-thin skulls of infants. I mean, insurgent Ihumpinstanian bundles of joy.

Flaming toddlers aside, we freed the fuck out of whoever the fuck they are/were. Huzzah! Purple Hearts and throbbing purple heads for the whole gang!

But it could not last. The salad days never do. Even salad days filled with hot meat. And not in a gay way.

My literary agent says the best way to whore myself out to supranational book publishing corporate pimps is to write a steamy steaming pile about conspiracies and Knights Templar conspiracies and mainstream trivialities posing as important topics and celebrities and whores. So I write that and it's called *A Dog Called Guano* which becomes a *New York Times* bestseller because of unparalleled anilingus.

In *A Dog Called Guano* I get discharged from my U.S. army death squad and end up in Los Angeles with some afro-wearing darky who is a leper who attaches a big snowplow-wedge to the front of his Oldsmobile in order to properly cut through L.A. gridlock. Why not? These superheroes for the modern age kill thousands of commuters but greatly improve traffic flow. Despite this, they run afoul of the State and its numerous supranational corporations. The California governor is a movie action hero and enlists a fellow movie action hero with thirty-pound testicles to help stop our furry and leprous antiheroes. Will they be captured and tortured in the spirit of America? Or will they detonate a nuclear device in the San Andreas Fault in order to trigger a magnitude 11 earthquake in order to topple all of Southern California into the ocean in order to have a happy ending? America is standing and cheering for the most hated book in America, *A Dog Called Guano.*

Sure sure, it's pathetic. Using this book that no one's read to pimp another book no one's read because of the Knights Templar conspiracy against me. Read on, dullard!

The leper and I eventually broke up. I don't think I ever really loved him. Sometimes you just get stuck in a relationship because you keep hoping that dogs can act as a leprosy carrier from one human to many, many other humans.

As if the U.S. army and a leper aren't bad enough: then I end up in Arizona.

Who is Oat Man?

Who the fuck cares.

Oatman is a town in Arizona. And I'm knee-deep in it.

Jealous?

In the town of Oatman, wild burros roam the dusty streets raping tourists. This makes humping human legs well-nigh impossible. Too much competition. You try humping the shank of some tubby housewife from Chicago while she's getting the ol' donkey bone. Won't even know you're there.

So through no fault of my own (it's never my fault because I'm a modern American) I'm out of work. The National Socialist German Workers' Party also known as the Animal Control Department also known as the Republican Party labels me a "stray." I prefer "well-hung freelancer."

Oatman: population 128. Not including sodomy-lovin' mules.

Half the population is cops. Because this is America: the finest police state this side of the many Third World police states America sponsors to suppress Third World drones resentful that their police state has been bribed to hand over its resources to First World police states such as Fortress America guarded in a prison-guard sense by both Republican and Democratic administrations in the finest democratic two-party dictatorship beholden to corporations this side of global capitalism.

The other half of the population is mildly retarded putting them intellectually above the cop-half of the population. Identical to the latest American census numbers.

Cop infestation. Mule infestation. Oatman: *a great place to live!* (cliché!)

Apprehension by the police state is imminent. According to the American census. According to the American census: Being dirt poor in modern capitalist society means I have only one good option: *join a good gang!* Unfortunately the Bloods, Crips, and various Islamic fundamentalist terror gangs are not hiring in Oatman. There's only the ass-raping burros.

So I join up.

My fighting weight is just under seventy pounds. So I'm a bit undersized for the jackass weight class. But I make up for it with my ginormous cock. As you know.

Most donkeys are brown or black. I am white. Advantage: Well-Endowed Aryan Cockmaster, purebred.

A lot of gangs have some sort of initiation ritual. Like making the novitiate drive at night without turning on the car headlights and then shooting the first asshole who responds by blinking their headlights which is the ritual the Shriners are famous for. Or making the novitiate hug some U.S. marines while wearing a plastique leisure suit. Or making the novitiate so poor he's forced to join the gang known as the U.S. marines in order to kill rival Third World gangs pissed off the marines are occupying their squalid Third World shithole in order to imperialize Third World shitholes and resources.

The donkeys make their novitiates perform autofellatio of which I'm a tenth-degree black belt (Grand Master…baiter. Ha!) After executing a perfect General Tso's Sweet-and-Spicy Anilingus while humming "The Old Master Painter from the Faraway Hills" I'm crowned president and order a war of conquest (being an American Guano). Two battalions of jackasses surround Oatman in a pincer movement. The northern prong catches the cops by surprise who are bent over and squeal like *pigs*. Ha! The southern prong penetrates the rear—*of many a tourist!*

My shock troops withdraw, bringing back booty. Cletus the mule reports: "Mr. El Presidente, our asses smoked their asses. Ha!"

El Presidente Guano: "Cletus the mule, you foul sodomite!"

Cletus the mule salutes by licking his mule cock.

"Don't let it go to your *head!*" I advise.

Admiral Neddy steps forward, salutes, and says with a mouthful of cock: "I am a rear admiral!"

Then I realize this homoerotic masterpiece was a Junior Samples skit on *Hee Haw*, Season Five, seen in syndication at the 2004 Republican Convention.

"Bring me the prisoners!" I command.

A donkey train drops its load. Then they drop their sacks: filled with *Snausages!*

With enough Snausages, I can:

A. $4.04
B. Rule the world.
C. Poison the world.
D. Binge and purge like a real supermodel.

Snausages are a precious pseudo-edible. Snausages futures are traded on the Chicago Board of Trade, you capitalist swine. Snausages are life™.

What else is one supposed to eat while holed up in a desolate mountain range? I hear bin Laden downs them by the fistful. (Source: Fox News)

Quarrelsome ass-rapemongering burros holed up in desolate mountains eat oats. Oats just, like, grow out of the ground and stuff. The mountains surrounding Oatman are filled with fields of oats. Duh.

I don't eat oats unless there are oats in these Snausages which I doubt because propylene glycol, titanium dioxide, yellow 5, and yellow 6 would gang up and kick the shit out of oats. And his fruity mustache. And Hall too, if there is a God. Which I doubt. Because any God couldn't hate me this much.

So I'm stuck in desolate mountains watching donkeys eating oats and their own cocks. I repeat: There is no God with an imagination powerful enough to hate me this much.

So then the super-colossal ass called Thomas L. Friedman starts braying mephitic spewings somehow even more noxious than usual, and then falls over. This is progress.

I command: "Quick! Get Thomas L. Friedman to his cloven hooves!"

The gang donkey punches Thomas L. Friedman which he has always enjoyed. As you know.

Thomas L. Friedman rises to his cloven hooves. He is a peculiar ass, preferring to speak out of his ass. This is the norm for humans but not for the more intelligent donkey species. Unless—

I charge Thomas L. Friedman and bite his ass. "The world is flat!" he farts from his ass. Instinctively I sink my canines in deep and shake my head back and forth. There's blood, more farting about the wonders of capitalism flattening the planet, and the tearing of cloth wondrously imported from some Third World shithole flattened by capitalism. The rear half of the two-man donkey costume rips away revealing: Thomas L. Friedman!

"As I suspected," I say, spitting out chunks of donkey costume and Thomas L. Friedman ass flaps. "We've been infiltrated by the womb broom of capitalism."

"Aye!" farts the critically acclaimed mongoloid in fruity mustache. "The womb broom of capitalism has penetrated your market!"

Excited to be manipulated by foreign capital, a thousand

and one donkeys gangbang the shit out of the womb broom of capitalism. Now full of indigenous ejaculate, previously full of shit, Thomas L. Friedman bulges and blows. As you know.

I'd clap. If I had hands.

Bits of exploded Thomas L. Friedman and donkey jizz are everywhere which I'll have to pay some Third World ass next to nothing to clean up.

"Halt! Who goes there?" I inquire of the front half of the Thomas L. Friedman jackass costume currently not exploded with hot donkey cum.

"It's me."

"Incorrect!" I correct. "Answer grammatically boldly with ''Tis I!'"

"'Tis I."

"'Tis who?"

"'Tis Pramod."

"Incorrect! I simply cannot have a central character named Ramrod. Wait. I've gone back and reread this manuscript. You're hired."

"Whatever you wish, sir."

"Exactly."

"Sir, may I inquire of you one question."

"The name of the manuscript is *A Dog Called Anal Fisting*."

"How is it, sir, I am speaking to a dog?"

"Because I am the divine vahana of Bhairava (the fierce manifestation of Shiva). So, um, don't fuck with me."

"I am no longer Hindu. I have converted to Christianity."

"Modern society is in certain respects extremely permissive. In matters that are irrelevant to the functioning of the system we can generally do what we please. We can believe in any religion we like (as long as it does not encourage behavior that is dangerous to the system)...We can do anything as long as it is *unimportant*. But in all *important* matters the system tends increasingly to regulate our behavior," says Uncle Ted

Kaczynski.

L. Sprague de Camp: "Today, in technologically advanced lands, men live very similar lives in spite of geographical, religious and political differences…These similarities are the result of a common technology…"

"So you see, my Ramrod, it really doesn't matter what religion you've converted to, you cock-sucking Christian sellout. Slave-religion motherfucker." I give him a dog-smile and a wink (*bing!*).

"That is wonderful, sir. I overflow with joy knowing the world will now only judge me on how vital a cog I am in the social machine."

"Don't forget the importance of judging others on their showy displays of wealth."

"I would not want to live in a world that was any other way, sir."

"Good man (oxymoron). So, what's a nice Third World turd like you doing in a place like this?"

"I am apprenticing under the Master Womb Broom."

"Oops. Guess it's time to find some new menial labor."

"I am deeply saddened to see the Master ruptured with hot pack-animal semen."

"It's the way he would have wanted to go." (Source: *The New York Times*)

"The Master was to market me as a capitalist-market success story in his new book *Outsource the Closet* after he fingered me in Mysore region. In India, sir."

"Bangalore, you say? Or was it *Bang galore*?"

"The Bangalore call center is known far and wide, in a global economic sense, for its Indian callboys."

"Specializing in *oral* work?"

"Yes, sir! Did I have the pleasure of previously servicing you?"

"For the *Siemens* Corporation, perchance?"

"I was trained to give the finest lip service."

"I'm sure that's why donkey balls over there, or over everywhere, took you under his wing, or under his something, or in his something, or all of the above, or $4.04."

"After being legally abducted from call-center cubicle, I was mailed to the United States. Here the Master began teaching me his Pulitzer Prize-winning mixed metaphors. And how to clean his laundry and the many peculiar stains.

"Then the Master's masters ordered him to go deep undercover under the cover of donkey costume to probe whether maximum-penetrating burros would be open to throbbing global capital. I assisted in getting his many peculiar stains out of the costume. It's a rental."

"Uh-oh. Looks like you're in danger of *blowing* your *deposit*."

I've finally had enough of the licentious but grotesque puns; I now end this filthy manuscript.

I'm a well-known liar.

Like I give two good shakes about your oh-so-decent sensibilities. Fucking clone.

I encourage my Ramrod to wear his half of Thomas L. Friedman's jackass costume at all times lest the rest of the jackasses figure out he's a Third World turd and employ him in a zipper factory.

"It is true that you're only masquerading as half an ass after the Thomas L. Friedman ass half detonated but the rest of the donkeys don't seem to care since the costume no longer has an ass half to hump which is all these asses care about anyway," I assure him. "So we're gonna attack Oatman at midnight and wipe it off the map. Wanna come?"

Ramrod is hesitant about committing genocide. I tell him he can just tag along and see if he can maybe catch a bus back to India.

"Oh, no, sir! I must follow the American Dream! I would sooner commit genocide than take a bus back to India."

"And that is the properly trademarked trademark of the American Dream."

He straps on the feedbag and considers nothing. Thus attaining the American Dream™.

"These oats are delicious," Ramrod chews while Cletus the mule sustainably drills Oatman's mayor's face holes with mule sperm. It's half past midnight and the genocide is going great. The Oatman City Council, in emergency session, has issued a none-too-gentle reproof of all genocidal activities not connected with American Imperialism™. Cletus the mule formally objects with a point of order. At Oatman High School, the gang is ballin' midnight basketball players. Down on Main Street, *shootout!* between actors dressed as Wild West gunslingers and donkey dominatrixes in leather and ball gags. The Oatman Whorehouse slashes prices on rim jobs and is overrun by bottom feeders from the orphanage. The Knights Templar join forces with the Freemasons and create conspiracies with the Bilderberg Group. Read on, American simpletons! A herd of tourists even more tumid than usual because they're Harley-Davidson bikers flatulate on their flatulent tumid machines. Harley-Davidson bikers (tourists of action) are individualistic rebels traveling in herds dressed in conforming uniforms of leather and American flags. Harley-Davidson bikers are somehow twice as morbidly obese as the average American. Tumid thighs that have never not rubbed each other in tight leather pants cause chafing and fires. "Sparks from chafed thighs of

Harley-Davidson tourists of action will ignite noxious gases spewing from tumid flatulating machines & tourists of action! (a necessary and entertaining means of population control!)" I bark as the Harley herd sparks & combusts.

A Harley biker spontaneously combusting

Listen: Harley-biker thigh friction igniting Harley-biker noxious gases is a renewable resource.

"Oh, the humanity!" I bark.

Listen: The American flag should never be burned unless a herd member is wearing it.

The Pit Of Your Stomach Bar & Grill may be the only place in Oatman where one can dine in a giant pit that animal carcasses are shoveled into. So it's an all-you-can-eat pit. This is popular with the Harley herd (individualistic rebel demographic) which, in feeding frenzy in pit, fails to notice they've burned down.

The fire is not contained in The Pit Of Your Stomach and spreads to The Second Amendment Munitions Pit next door. It's like the Fourth of July with all the exploding munitions and American flags and biker individualists. I'd clap if I had hands. So I pick up a charred tumid Harley-biker hand. Start your own collection today!

Everything is going according to plan. Obviously. Then a hundred-yard puddle of shit oozes out from the bus station. Don't get me wrong. It *is* a nice complement to the festivities. But it's not in the plan. I went back and checked. And without a plan, any genocide will end up disappointing.

I pick up four feet and slide them on my paws. Only a fool purchases galoshes with all the free ones hanging off tumid Harley bikers. And they're made in America which one can take civic pride in. I slosh through the shitty bus station only to find: *my Ramrod!*

"Well, my Ramrod has been in worse places," I bark to myself. "Then again, I'm a well-known liar."

"Hello, sir," says the front half of the Thomas L. Friedman donkey costume.

"My Ramrod, my Ramrod, what have ye done?" Throughout the bus station lay pack animals replete with explosive diarrhea.

"I was waiting for the bus, sir."

"Don't get me wrong—I love what you've done with the place. I saw the groaning-donkeys-laying-in-their-own-liquefied-excrement motif was featured in last month's *Maison and Serf.* A Condé Nast jewel."

Ramrod looks at me and chews oats from his feedbag.

"How do you eat oats from a feedbag with that donkey head over your head?"

"I have an eighteen-inch prehensile tongue."

"Christ! You're the next step in the human evolutionary

process. Once we figure out a way to sell this on eBay our troubles will be over!"

Toot toot! Ramrod lets out a lil' flatulence. Seven donkey gangsters downwind of his ass convulse, collapse, and squirt shit all over themselves.

"Once we figure out a way to sell this on eBay our troubles will be over!"

"These all-natural, locally grown oats are delicious, sir. But they make me a little gassy."

"This is a blatant ripoff of The Spleen's flatulence super-power from *Mystery Men*. Try again."

Ramrod, being the hideous Indian bastard in half a donkey costume that he is, chants: "By the power vested in me by the state of life-giving, high-fiber oats: *Om!*" An O-shaped, oat-colored shock wave pulses from him. Anything within a hundred-yard radius complies by convulsing, collapsing, and squirting shit all over itself.

"I am only a corridor through which the life-giving, high-fiber power of oats flows," Ramrod explains. "Feel the power of regularity."

"Make that *super*-regularity," I explain as the pool of diarrhea floods Main Street. "Causing living creatures to convulse, collapse, and shit all over themselves is your God-given super-power. Once we figure out a way to sell this on eBay and to the U.S. military our troubles will be over!"

"I must learn how to control this mighty force within me. I fear it is the reason the Master Womb Broom convulsed and collapsed just before being inseminated by a thousand and one donkeys."

"Yes yes. Thank God your super-power works on asses of all species."

"Except on you, sir. You remain in-incontinent, which by my super-power of deduction means you are continent."

"It's all the Snausages. I'm now immune to bowel

movements."

The midnight bus to Los Angeles skids through the excrement and opens its door. "Los Angeles: a city that honestly enjoys being mired in its own filth. You should fit right in there."

"But, sir, I am afraid they will take advantage of me. Will you not come with me and take advantage of me?"

"Of course. Being a rancid parasite who creates nothing of value while feeding off other's talents and hard work is defined as capitalist. You know, you bleating nationalistic sheep: the American Dream!"™

Best-case scenario, I'd pimp the kid to the entertainment industry: the power to make people shit all over themselves should make an especially popular reality TV show. Worst-case scenario, I'd sell the kid into slavery or to the coprophagia department of the porno industry.

You know, you bleating nationalistic sheep: the American Dream!

I call my agent. I tell him I'm about to turn Los Angeles into a bigger steaming pile than it already is and inquire if he would help me sell the shit out of it. Ha! He cums all over himself, wipes up, and gets me an interview with some corporate executive pimp at some supranational media steaming pile corporation.

In order to look like a superhero my Ramrod wears half a donkey costume. And on the donkey's forehead we've stitched an oat-colored "O" which stands for something mysterious. "Long after we've whored this show into the ground for all the advertising money we can whore up, we'll reveal what the 'O' stands for," I tell the corporate executive pimp I'm pimping this steaming pile show idea to. He likes the sound of all that. Naturally. "Now give us some gobs of cash, corporate pimp."

"Wait," says pimp. "I need to see a demonstration of Oat Man's super-power before we all whore this thing out for gobs of cash."

"Sure sure," I bark. I command of my Ramrod: "Give him The Big O."

"By the power vested in me by the state of life-giving, high-fiber oats: *Om!*" Then, nothing. No corporate pimp blowing explosive diarrhea all over the conference room more than usual.

I ask pimp: "You on the South Beach Snausages Diet?"

"Ha! Hahahahahahahahahaha!" hohos pimp. The merciless whoremaster pulls from his Armani suit an Armani electric hot-glue gun with Armani extension cord.

"Put the gun down!" I bark!

Fourteen armed corporate lapdogs barge in and hold Ramrod down while pimp glues an "L" made of real felt to his donkey forehead. The company henchmen throw Ramrod out a window. I take the elevator.

Twenty stories later I'm on the ground. I run to Ramrod. Actually, more like a trot. "Plenty of buses leaving L.A. for India, you abject failure," I bark.

"I am sorry, sir. I cannot explain my power outage."

"Aha! Maybe it's because of this!" I bark and pull from his donkey costume pocket a package of Ye Olde Third World Sweatshoppe Oats.

"I apologize, sir. Their Wal-Mart price is unbeatable."

"You are fortunate the falls of Third World turds are often broken by Third World turd ground forces." The Indian nods and gets up off the pack of Mexicans. A smashed leaf blower wheezes a death rattle.

Once my agent hears of this catastrophe he'll hire a helicopter equipped with Sarah Palin to shoot me down and feed my carcass to her retarded offspring. No, wait. Her retarded offspring devour factory-farmed carcasses shoveled into their pit.

My carcass will be left to rot. As usual.

I'm on the next bus back to Oatman. No one in their right mind would ever venture there. A good place to hide out. Bin Laden has a summer home there.

I tried to send Ramrod back to India but the bus fare was too expensive.

He removes his donkey head and asks, "What does the 'L' on my forehead stand for?"

"Winner."

For the record, the "L" is glued next to the "O" which spells LO which stands for winner. We stitch on an exclamation point after the letters which spells LO! which gives his donkey forehead that ol' timey Biblical feel.

Most of Oatman burned down after the donkey attack so looks better than usual. We wade through the liquefied excrement always found in bus stations and retreat to the hills.

"What now, sir?"

"I don't know about you, but I'm gonna get knee-deep in Snausages."

"Sir, the Master Womb Broom of Capitalism and the rest of the indoctrination spewing from society's large institutions (e.g., supranational media corporations, supranational corporate tyrannies of all beautiful colors and creeds, the 'education' system, government in general) teach that in an impossible situation one must obey the rules laid down by society's large institutions and not revolt in any meaningful way that jeopardizes large institutions."

"And thus live the American Dream! Amen, backward brown brother! We will persevere and fight on! And get our own reality TV show!" I bark!

So, being an individual facing an untenable situation due to society's large institutions, I do what society's sheep are indoctrinated to do: get a lawyer and call a press conference.

Oatman's local TV station, WOAT, owned by a supranational media corporation, is live, local, and late breaking!™

"I've called this press conference today to announce that my cock is huge," I bark. "In other news!—" On cue, degenerate ass-marauding burros crash through the windows.

Here's the backstory: A gang of ass-harrying burros had been harrying the town of Oatman throughout this chapter. Here's the backstory on gangs: An oppressive world economic scheme in which 2 percent of the planet's population owns over 50 percent of the planet's wealth spawns gangs when some of the slightly brighter segments of the 50 percent of the world's population that owns 0 percent of the world's wealth begin to realize they're wholly fucked. A criminal enterprise with state backing is called a corporation. Socioeconomic dead ends with no state backing are called cheap labor. To escape this, socioeconomic dead ends must cooperate in the schemes selling drugs, gambling, whores, and slaves that do not have state backing. Corporations are called state-backed enterprises selling drugs, gambling, whores, and slaves. Contact your authorities for details. The similar scheme of selling rabid religious fundamentalism provides a sense of camaraderie, identity, and self-esteem to socioeconomic dead ends who have little self-esteem because they understand they're socioeconomic dead ends. But it's better to oppress the shit out of and declare never-ending war against Islamic terror gangs than give up stealing their resources in order to allow them real economic opportunities so they would have far less inclination to join Islamic terror gangs. Contact your authorities for details.

Pay the fuck attention: Controlling sheep is best done by way of a pervasive culture of fear. Ass-diddling terror burros are scary and begin with the letter A and thus should be linked with Al-Qaeda.

"Holy smegma!" I bark into the press conference microphone. "Ass-diddling burros are this week's Hitler or Ho Chi Minh or Manuel Noriega or Ayatollah Khomeini or Castro or Colonel Gaddafi or Jim J. Bullock!" The terrified press corps agrees and begins diddling their own asses in a preemptive strike against the burros. "The terrified press corps promotes the basic worldview of the National Security State! This is handy when fear mongering the drones and clones into their customary state of catatonia."

"The whole aim of practical politics is to keep the populace alarmed (and hence clamorous to be led to safety) by menacing it with an endless series of hobgoblins, all of them imaginary," newspaperman H.L. Mencken wrote a century ago but couldn't have written today since Mencken's best insights are far too misanthropically brilliant for the unctuous sensibilities of any modern mainstream newspaper and its underdeveloped readership.

"Christ! Look at the hobgoblins on that one!" I bark into

the microphone as Long Dong Silver Burro's testicles bounce on the forehead of a press corps member. Get it? Press corps *member*? Ha!

The smell of K-Y Jelly and press corps smegma permeates the Oatman Elementary School romper room. As usual.

The Oatman Elementary School romper room is where I hold my press conferences because of the often-pornographic content. Of the romper room. Demented anal-yzing donkeys lay their testicles on the press corps like the laying on of hands. "Only yet another superhero promoting the basic worldview of the National Security State can save us now!" I bark into microphone. On cue, yet another jackass crashes through a window. Only this jackass makes up for its missing ass with "LO!" emblazoned on its forehead because it's: *Oat Man!*

Through oat feedbag Oat Man announces: "By the power vested in me by the state of life-giving, high-fiber oats: *Om!*" O-shaped, oat-colored shock wave pulses from him. Pack animals & press corps convulse, heehaw, collapse, and squirt shit all over themselves. He concludes, "Feel the power of regularity!"

"Make that *super*-regularity," I bark into microphone as pool of diarrhea rises from pool of reporters. "Heehawing and shitting all over oneself is a popular long-standing tradition among Americans. And now it's a powerful new weapon in America's never-ending War on Terror, War on Drugs, and War on Christmas. Once we figure out a way to sell this to a major TV network our troubles will be over!"

From the pool of feculence comes: "Oat Man! Oat Man! Trix Lexis, WOAT Action Infarction Action News here! Now that you've left the terrorists and press wallowing in their own poo, what are you going to do next?"

"I'm going to Disneyland!"

"You fool!" I bark into the microphone. "What Oat Man *means* to say is we are open to whoring ourselves out to whichever fascist supranational corporate media gang gives us the largest gob of cash; and our own reality TV show. If Disney wants Oat Man to fuck their rat, on TV, they'd better get on the horn real quick, 'cause we got options. Make no mistake: we are gonna get balls deep in the biggest supranational corporate rat with the biggest sack. Of cash."

Excretion asks: "Oat Man! What's your Twitter name?"

"@just-another-modern-know-nothing-narcissistic-enough-to-believe-my-constant-brainless-electronic-flatuses-about-my-daily-minutiae-and-all-other-trivialities-should-be-made-public-in-140-characters-or-less-because-my-thoughtful-observations-on-life-never-would-require-more-than-140-characters-anyway."

Egesta: "Oat Man! Tell us who the man behind the front half of the donkey costume really is!"

"Pramod Cāpalūsa Gudā Mukha."

"That means 'Lick my Ramrod' in the Aryan tongue. Because only a white man could impersonate this powerful an ass. Ask Thomas L. Friedman," I bark into the microphone. "Remember: this is no cheap made-in-the-Third-World action figure who will give spoiled First World brats cadmium poisoning after they're finished consuming him, I mean sucking him. Sorry. Slip of the *tongue*. Ha!"

"Oat Man! What does the 'LO!' stand for?"

"*Wiener!*"

Sure sure. I set up the donkeys to take a fall. They weren't getting their own reality TV show anytime soon. So I tell the dumb beasts about all the fresh ass cruising Oatman Elementary, then schedule the media lackeys. The hardest thing was coaching up my Ramrod. There's only so much I can do with such limited human talent (redundant). But he stayed in character and left 'em heehawing and shitting all over themselves which is always a TV ratings winner.

But before we get a facial full of gobs of cash the TV network pimps want to see the concept onscreen and order a pilot episode to be shot of *Oat Man: The Fiber of America*. The series premiere centers on a Catechist Kiddie Molosser—purebred, AKC registered—and his Ramrod in half donkey suit holding an open audition to find other superheroes so they can form a gang of superheroes. See preceding gang definition for details.

We hold the audition in Oatman Elementary because gangs like schools.

The director jumps up and down and screams "*Action, action, action!*" In walks some guy in a janitor's outfit.

I dog-whine, "This is the best we can do?"

"I'm told superheroes have come from as far away as Needles, California," promises my Ramrod.

Dogs can cry tears of misery and abject despair as any dog who spends time with humans will attest. "What is your super-name and super-power?" I'll ask the janitor if I can get enough soma down my gullet to endure and medicate away this modern existence.

"I am the Trash Can Do! Man!" he announces.

"What is your super-power, Trash Can Do! Man?" asks my Ramrod, somehow genuinely interested.

"My superhero power is taking the trash thrown by litterers and stuffing it down their throats!" Then a bunch of cops barge in and beat and taser and beat Trash Can Do! Man. "He was fine as long as he concentrated on the droves of Mexican litterers. Because this is Arizona," one cop tells our camera. "But when he stuffed methyl isocyanate and other toxins from Bhopal,

India down the shareholders' throats of the Dow Chemical Corporation, then the justice system swings into action!" says the cop swinging the baton into Trash Can Do! Man's head.

"When you're done serving your thousand-year stretch in Attica, call me," I tell all the finest superheroes as they're dragged and beaten out the door.

Next up is some guy wearing the front half of a two-man mule costume. "Uh-oh. Competition," I tell the half jackass sitting beside me. "I'll finally be able to outsource your Indian ass back to Bhopal."

"I'm from Bangalore, sir."

"I love it when you talk dirty."

"I am The Mule!" announces The Mule. "My superhero power is the ability to carry a burdensome cargo. However, I can carry less than heavy machinery can, making The Mule outmoded. So I've revamped my superhero power to carry ninety condoms full of heroin in my digestive tract." Then the police state barges in and beats and tasers and beats The Mule out the door before I can hire him.

Next up is some guy wearing the back half of a two-man jackass costume. "The Master Womb Broom has risen!" brays my Ramrod!

"Or it's the back half of The Mule chock-full o' heroin condoms! We're saved!" I bark!

"Nay!" brays ass. "It is me! The Paronomasiac: teller of powerful puns!"

"We're saved!" I bark!

The Paronomasiac mounts my Ramrod; and are now one. "*Heehaw!*" Oat Man's ass heehaws. "I'd be an ass*whole* if I wasn't so *half*-assed!"

"Pun-derful! We're saved!" I bark!

Next up is the Amazing Gentrification-Man and his sidekick the Fantastic Slumlord.

Fantastic Slumlord: "Oatman, Arizona! What a dump!"

Amazing Gentrification-Man: "What an opportunity!"

The toilet leaks.

Fantastic Slumlord: "Put a towel around it."

The roof leaks.

Fantastic Slumlord: "Stand under it and say *ah*. That's filtered water!"

The front door doesn't work.

Fantastic Slumlord: "Use a window."

I'm behind on your illegitimate rent.

Fantastic Slumlord: "Meet my wacky sidekick, the sheriff. And his sidekick, the eviction."

Then Amazing Gentrification-Man swoops in (heroically) to buy Fantastic Slumlord's shithole, throws some spackle up, and sells it to upwardly mobile, cultureless-yet-soulless yuppies for gobs of cash. Then the evictee drinks filtered water through the upwardly mobile yuppies' spacious home-theater-system cardboard box in the alley.

"Well you wouldn't want an economic system where those who use and occupy a piece of land are the only legitimate owners of that land!" I bark!

"Using illegitimate land titles to charge the peasantry illegitimate rent and illegitimately evict their asses in order to sell the land to hoarders of capital is just *super*!" farts Thomas L. Friedman or the Paronomasiac: you decide!

"You're hired!" I bark.

The Amazing Gentrification-Man: "Sorry. I already star in my own reality TV show: *Flip That Foreclosure Scam* on The Learning Channel. No, really. They actually call it The Learning Channel!"

"Ha!" I bark!

"Ha!" TV network pimps ha-ha.

"I guess he told us to *flip* off!" heehaws Oat Man's ass.

Next up is a six-foot ear of genetically modified corn riding in on a cow.

"You're hired!" I bark!

"I am The Man!santo!" corn announces. "Cultured freshly in The Man!santo Corporation laboratories daily!" The Man!santo claps his hands which are nozzles attached to arms which are hoses made of the latest genetically modified edible plastic™. The Man!santo is excited and ejaculates from his nozzles Roundup herbicide which is cherished by millions of fat American imbeciles too fat 'n lazy to bend over to dig up weeds by hand and causes the death of human embryonic, placental, and umbilical cells *in vitro*, even at low concentrations.

"You're hired!" I bark!

"I am The Man!santo! I ride my trusty steed, the Dow *Kapow!* Cow!" The cow looks at me and squirts blood from its eyeballs. The Man!santo claps 'n squirts from his nozzles rBGH (recombinant Bovine Growth Hormone) which The Man!santo then sells to pharmaceutical Superuncle Eli & Superaunt Lilly for three hundred million dollars.

"You're hired!" I bark!

The Dow *Kapow!* Cow has a hole in its middle where a big-screen TV is implanted. The big-screen TV is a sweet seventy-inch plasma so I'd clap if I had hands. And The Man!santo claps his nozzles. Playing on the Dow *Kapow!* Cow Channel is that Dow commercial with that friendly, caring narrator's voice voicing:

For each of us, there's a moment of discovery

Unless you're talking about the discovery process in the "justice" system because there was no discovery for the maimed and deformed Vietnamese Agent Orange victims suing Dow and Man!santo for their production of Agent Orange which contained dioxin, a known poison, because the U.S. courts refused to hear the lawsuit because the plaintiffs were just some fucked up Vietnamese, so, no, for each of us there's not necessarily a moment of discovery especially when you consider how dim the average American is but that's going off on a whole other tangent

We understand that all of life is elemental

Like the element plutonium, the radioactive waste of which ended up in the air and water when Dow managed the Rocky Flats nuclear weapons production facility in Colorado

And as we marvel at element bonding with element (also called nuclear fusion which makes marvelous hydrogen bombs—see Dow's marvelous record at Rocky Flats) *we soon realize that when you add the human element to the equation, everything changes* (unless you're asking Dow to change and clean up its toxins in Bhopal that murdered 20,000 human elements (390 tons of toxic chemicals abandoned at the pesticide plant still continue to leak and pollute the groundwater in the region and affect thousands of Bhopal residents who depend on it) because when you add those Bhopal human elements to the Dow equation it equals no cleanup money, bitch)

Suddenly, all of chemistry illuminates humanity (video of Dow-produced napalm *illuminating* some Third World yokels)

And all of humanity illuminates chemistry (whatever that nonsensical flatulence is supposed to mean—hell, show video of some Dow subhumans mixing up all those plastics and poisons that make modern life just swell while also making planetary life swell, and rupture; or just show video of an illuminating mushroom cloud from a hydrogen bomb from Rocky Flats)

The human element: nothing is more fundamental, nothing more elemental

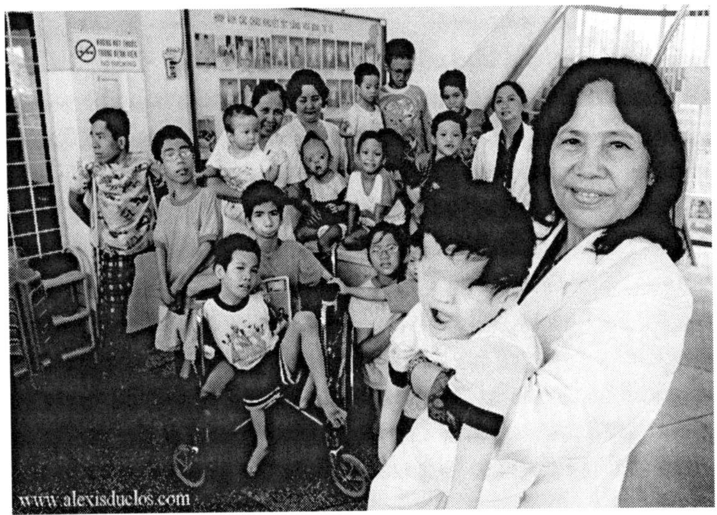

Handicapped children, most of them Agent Orange victims: a small part of Dow's humble homage to the human element. (photo courtesy of AlexisDuclos.com via Wikipedia.org)

"Wow. By its very nature this evil system creates a lot of rotten fuckers, but The Man!santo and Dow, *these* two oozing chancres...*Christ!* Not even for my own reality show will I wade in their cesspool," I bark. "You're fired!" I bark!

The Man!santo squeals and squirts from his nozzles genetically modified Roundup-resistant canola oil. The TV network pimps send in some of their whores to wrestle each other in a pool of genetically modified Roundup-resistant canola oil in string bikinis.

"The American Dream!™" hails my Ramrod.

"Our TV ratings will be through the roof!" I bark! "We're saved!"

So we're pretty well fucked. As usual. The audition netted us one pun-farting ass augmentation for my Ramrod. Not exactly a *gang* of superheroes. So it's on to Plan B which is panic. Then Plan C kicks in which is wander around the streets chasing pussy. "Get it? *Chasing pussy?* Because he's a *dog!*" Oat Man's ass farts.

The best we can find is some half-incoherent old man and a drunk Indian (redundant). So after getting all up in dat sweet ass we sign them on as indentured servants, the industry standard.

"They died for your freedom!" our wise old man yells from the sidewalk at passing motorists.

"He believes every day is Veterans Day. Or Memorial Day. Or Independence Day. Or Armed Forces Day. Or The State Is Laughing At You Brainwashed Jingoistic Flag-Sucking Militaristic Know-Nothing Slaves Day. I can't remember which one. 'Cause I'm a drunk Indian."

"That's OK," I console him. "Here, have another sip of this rubbing alcohol, chief."

He wisely listens to my advice and downs the bottle. "Ah! That is indeed better."

"Refreshing, eh, chief?"

"Yes. It keeps the red man down."

"Don't I know it, chief," I bark, pawing the six-pack of nail polish remover.

"The white man's firewater is a weapon. It keeps him in control and us powerless."

"Don't I know it, chief," I bark, pawing the shiny trinkets, smallpox-infested blankets, fraudulent land-for-peace deals, designer jeans, big-screen televisions, latest gotta-have techno gadgets, shiny trinkets, luxury automobiles.

"Speak English! This is America!" yells wise old man.

"Wow. This is great. The only thing drunk Indian and wise old man are missing are superhero costumes," I bark. And so our first superhero mission is to find our hot new additions superhero garb. And so we go into the Oatman alley. There, in order to steal the homeless wino's robe, we must first sexually molest him. Naturally. "Here, wise old man. Try on this robe that has been pre-saturated with urine for your protection," I bark. We wrestle the robe onto wise old man over his super-absorbent undergarment, saturated with urine for his protection. "You now look wise, wise old man. That is a standard men's size, limited-edition Harry Potter robe. Join the struggle against the evil Lord Voldemort. Become Harry Potter and team up with your friends Ron Weasley and Hermione Granger to save the Muggle world from the Dark Lord. 100% polyester."

"Only in America!" yells wise old man at traffic.

We molest and steal the clothes of the drunk Indian in the alley and give them to our own drunk Indian. Native American feather headdress, fringed tassel boots, breechcloth: all pre-vomited on.

"A moral dilemma: Should we light these homeless folks on fire?" I bark to myself. "No no. Oatman Elementary will be letting out within the hour. Some ambitious fourth-grader destined for military service or Wall Street will do it."

We retreat to the hills. With reality show camera crew in tow. Naturally. "Now that we are a gang of superheroes, we need a superhero lair," I bark to all the stupid fuckers following me. "You stupid fuckers."

"Would it be possible to find a vacant Batcave in the vicinity, sir?" Oat Man asks.

"Possibly. But the Batcave owner will not rent it to a dot

head. Sorry. That's the law. And for good reason. Better let me do the talking," I bark.

We wander through some more oat fields to the mouth of an abandoned mine. Oat Man peers into the pitch-black aperture. "It's too dark. I can see nothing down this shaft, sir." I ram my broad brick-like forehead into his back. But only after getting a running start. Oat Man and his ass tumble into the hole. A few minutes later the rest of us on the surface hear him hit bottom. I bark to Oat Man: "Watch your step. It could be a long drop down."

"I am OK, sir!"

"Never mind that. Is there anything down there we can steal or hump?" I bark.

"The shaft is a straight drop down for four hundred yards. I am unharmed, sir, but I do believe I have broken my ass."

"I guess those are the *breaks! Heehaw!*" heehaws Oat Man's ass.

"There is a rickety wooden ladder from the mouth of the mine all the way down, sir."

"That is very interesting!" I bark to him. "He's doomed. Let's get the fuck out of here," I bark to the others.

"America: Love it or leave it!" agrees wise old man.

"No. We cannot leave donkey man in mine," slurs drunk Indian.

"Yes we can!" I bark as an American flag flies proudly from my asshole.

"We must help donkey man," drunk Indian ridiculously holds.

"You Indians are always standing up for each other. That's your problem as a race. I can only say that because it's true and I'm white," I bark.

"The white man's burden! God bless America!" agrees wise old man.

"Lookit, this has nothing to do with the fact that you and he are mud people," I bark. "I mean, golly! For centuries, whitey has been the planet's arch-criminal in terms of economic malfeasance, environmental malefaction, and having a thimbledick. And golly again! In this modern age of homogenization, everyone working for the system is now a whitey. Which means *billions* of *whiteys!* Even if they're mud people on the outside, they're now all-whitey on the inside—where it counts!" I bark as red, white, and blue fireworks proudly launch from my asshole.

"United we stand!" agrees wise old man.

"Criminal whitey's worldwide criminal system feeding off a criminal human overpopulation explosion neatly crowd out the other life forms on the planet. I mean, an evil unsustainable system of seven billion huminions has led to the worst spate of planetary extinctions since the dinosaurs vanished sixty-five million years ago, according to the United Nations Convention on Biological Diversity."

"Go forth and multiply!" agrees wise old man.

"Moral of the story: Don't worry about the one huminion lost in a hole because your kind will make more."

"That's the magic of our free market system!" agrees wise old man.

"Sure sure. It's a *capitalist* market, not a *free* market. A *truly free* market is not manipulated by large concentrations of capital with state backing (e.g., price fixing, collusion, special deals, hidden subsidies, tax breaks…). In an economy organized around a *real* free market, exchange is between producers, and production is carried out mainly by self-employed artisans and farmers, small producers' cooperatives, worker-controlled large enterprises, and consumers' cooperatives. In a *truly free* market, all the costs of production would be borne by the producer. Not like in your *capitalist* market, where large concentrations of capital (corporations) use the State to deflect the costs of production onto the public (in economics, this is called *cost externalizing*). But do keep calling yours a *free* market. The billions and billions are too dim to look beyond your spurious definitions anyway. This is wonderful black humor," I bark.

Drunk Indian: "We cannot leave donkey man."

"Oh, poopy!" I bark.

I ram drunk Indian, wise old man, and reality show camera crew into the hole and jump in. Drunk Indian, wise old man, and camera crew break my fall four hundred yards later.

The most important thing to remember is that the TV camera remains unharmed.

"They made the ultimate sacrifice so you could speak English!" yells wise old man.

The light on the TV camera cuts through the darkness to reveal: *a mine tunnel!*

"The most important thing to remember is that the TV camera and I must remain unharmed!" I bark!

The TV camera pans slowly down the mine tunnel to reveal leaping and snorting out of the darkness: *Hellevator!*

BLACKNESS

GRAPHIC BURNS IN:

One of the Mass Media's

Supranational Corporate Steaming Piles

Presents

GRAPHIC SIZZLES OUT.

GRAPHIC BURNS IN:

A Steaming Pile Production

GRAPHIC FIZZLES OUT.

A piercing WHINE is building on the soundtrack. Then suddenly from out of the blackness rises AN ELEVATOR! A SLOW ZOOM brings it towards us. And as the whine reaches its sharp crescendo the elevator's doors spring open to reveal: BIG SHARP SCARY TEETH! BIG FLAMING FIREBALLS AFLAME! GROSS OOZE and possibly even SALIVA! with the graphic "HELLEVATOR!!!!!!!!" speeding straight out of the teeth and flames and spit IN 3-D! straight out into the audience so it seems to really jump right out at them which'll be scary.

CUT TO:

EXT. SHANGRI-LA — LUNCHTIME

It is a beautiful day in PARADISE. A light breeze blows through FIELDS OF GOLD. The theme music is Sting's DULCET "Fields of Gold," the song's rights having been acquired by our particular supranational corporate steaming pile along with Sting's marvelous genitals. A HELICOPTER SHOT sweeps to the middle of the golden field where a golden light emanates from a Vulvar Cheeselike Sebaceous Secretion Retriever, PUREBRED. There, in PARADISE, in the middle of FIELDS OF GOLD, the illuminated canine licks HIS marvelous genitals. A HELICOPTER SHOT sweeps over his GINORMOUS cock which is a turgid GOLDEN fire hose which speeds straight out at the audience IN 3-D! The scene is serene and softly suspended. A graphic appears over this idyllic image: "STARRING: GUANO!!!!!!!!!!" which speeds straight out at the audience IN 3-D! with theme music from *Raiders of the Lost Ark* blaring.

GRAPHIC BURNS IN:

The End

A dramatic pause, then question marks burn in so GRAPHIC reads:

The End??????????

which speeds straight out at the audience IN 3-D!

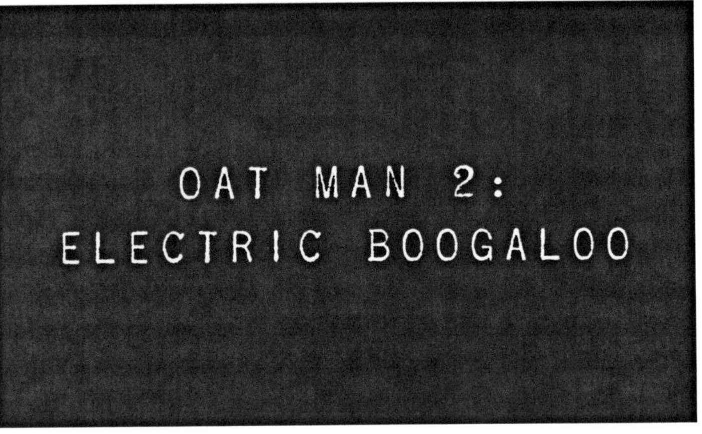

OAT MAN 2: ELECTRIC BOOGALOO

Dear corporate executive pimps:

A two-page screenplay can be expanded by adding various scenes showing close-up full penetration. Now as agreed, slather me in gobs of cash.

Hellevator! leaps and snorts out of the darkness. I step forward (heroically). “Everyone, take shelter under my GINORMOUS cock!” I bark! “That was one *helluva* (ha!) heroic line I just did. Are you rolling the TV camera?”

An audible *ding!* dings from Hellevator! Its infernal doors open revealing big scary teeth, fireballs, forked tongue (in director’s cut only), spittle, and: the television camera crew of *Flip That Foreclosure Scam* on The Learning Channel!

“Of course!” I bark! “And that can only mean one thing: We’re behind on the rent to this dump!”

“Indeed!” cackles the Fantastic Slumlord and his wacky sidekick the sheriff and his sidekick the eviction. “And I’ve got some illegal Chinese immigrants lined up who'll pay through the nose to move into a hazardous mine!"

"And that can only mean one thing!" I bark!

"Indeed!" cackles the Amazing Gentrification-Man. "I've got some cultureless-yet-soulless yuppies lined up who'll pay top dollar to move into a hazardous mine after I swoop in (heroically) to buy Fantastic Slumlord's shithole and throw some spackle up! (The yuppies will pay bottom dollar to keep the illegal Chinese on as the help since they have a wealth of experience working for next to nothing in hazardous mining operations.)"

"And I'm proud to be an American, where at least I know I'm free! And I won't forget the men who died, who gave that right to me!" agrees wise old man underneath my ginormous cock.

"Then *this* is the America Dream! I have found it!" rejoices Oat Man.

"Yes, my son. You have found it. Your flat-earth journey is at an end," the spirit of the Master Womb Broom of Capitalism farts.

The Amazing Gentrification-Man warmly puts his arm around my Ramrod and whispers into his ear and puts his tongue into his ear: "You see, Oat Man, the reason I auditioned for your superhero gang was to keep tabs on superheroes who might interfere with my plan to gentrify the shithole of Oatman."

"Thank you, sir, for exposing yourself to me," thanks Oat Man.

"But wait, there's more!" I bark!

Hellevator dings and opens its doors and vomits up: *The Man!santo riding the Dow* Kapow! *Cow!*

"As I suspected!" I bark!

"As you suspected!" ear of genetically modified corn agrees, claps its hands which are nozzles, and squirts rBGH, PCBs, and DDT in the good ol' LOL (Land Of Liberty (LOL!))!

"With age comes wisdom!" yells wise old man.

"And I would have gotten away with it if it weren't for you meddling kids!" squeals The Man!santo.

"And I would have gotten away with it if it weren't for you meddling kids!" yells wise old man.

The pilot episode director jumps up and down and screams "*Action, action, action!*"

Through oat feedbag Oat Man announces to the camera: "By the power vested in me by the state of life-giving, high-fiber—"

"No no no no no no no!" scream director and TV corporate pimps. "You cannot compel a corporate sponsor steaming pile to squirt shit all over themselves!"

The corporate sponsor steaming pile known as The Man!santo squeals and claps his hands which are nozzles and squirts out a legion of blood-snorting lawyers. "We are legion," lawyers claim in the copy of the complaint legally served upon us. "You will pay The Man!santo's Technology Fee!"

"The Man!santo Technology Fee is the fee any and all must pay to use The Man!santo's genetically engineered products," I bark.

Oat Man is confused; as usual. And chews oats. Under my ginormous cock.

"My Ramrod, I shall tell ye a story," I bark. "Once upon a time there was a big blight known as The Man!santo upon the even bigger blight known as humanity. The Man!santo's pastimes included evil and evil. Then one day The Man!santo's comprehensive fleet of genetically modified organisms used the wind to cross-pollinate with other crops. Organic farms found their pure food had been contaminated with genetically modified DNA thus ruining their businesses. Causing The Man!santo to cackle and ejaculate chemicals. After ejaculating, The Man!santo ejaculated his legion of blood-snorting lawyers upon innocent farmers whose crops had been cross-pollinated with The Man!santo's genetically modified pollen because innocent farmers who never wanted The Man!santo's genetically engineered crimes against nature were now criminals. You see, The Man!santo had patented the genetically modified organisms that infiltrated the farmers' natural crops, making the farmers guilty of patent infringement, according to the perverse System's perverse patent system. Since their crops now had the genetic mark of The Man!santo (666) they were responsible for paying The Man!santo tribute. The Man!santo's tribute being gobs and gobs of cash. Naturally. This naturally applies to all plants worldwide, according to the perverse System's perverse patent and 'free trade' systems."

Oat Man is stupefied; as usual. And thus attains the American Dream. Under my ginormous cock.

"O hark! my stupefied Ramrod: The Man!santo and legion claim in the copy of the complaint legally served upon us that the wild oat fields growing around Oatman and elsewhere and everywhere have been infected with their patented genetically 'n monstrously modified oats. Here's betting the genetically modified oats caused a mutation in your DNA structure giving you the super-power of super-regularity and giving the vast majority of others the super-power of cancerous tumors. Every time you ingest wild oats and make others squirt shit on themselves you owe The Man!santo gobs of cash, according to the System's perverse patent, 'free trade,' and 'justice' systems."

The police state barges in and beats and tasers and beats Oat Man. "Welcome to the American Dream™, patented by The Man!santo Corporation et al. When you're done serving your thousand-year stretch in Attica, call me," I tell all the finest superheroes as they're beaten and dragged and beaten out the mine.

GRAPHIC BURNS IN:

The End!!!!!!!!!!!!!!!!

which speeds straight out at the audience IN 3-D!

One of the cops who beat and tasered and beat my Ramrod decided he was in the market for a Beverly Hills Chihuahua Copulator, purebred, and adopted me and told me a bedtime story:

She unconsciously stroked the bottle of caffeinated low-carb malt liquor beverage which was enjoyed by all the most splendid young professionals, and not so long ago drunk by only the most desperate homeless offscourings. She could think of but one thing. The object of her affection.

It was not his looks that drew her to him; they were average. It was not his style of dress—although trendy, he lacked that ineffable panache which separated the pretenders from the truly gilded. It was certainly not his personality, for she had not met him yet, and it wouldn't have made a difference had she known him forever—a *good personality* was something charitably consigned to the misshapen.

It was none of these things that had her falling in love. It was something transcendent. Something indefatigably passionate. Something contemporary.

It was his cell phone.

Pressed firmly to ear, engaged in conversation, she had spied the cellular treasure and its human carrying case the moment they strolled into the lounge, as had anyone else with taste.

She was smitten with a fevered ardor. In this moment of rapture, all else faded from the scene's canvas, leaving only him. There alone, her talking *mondain* stood, bathed in the most heavenly light; his features softly accentuated under the ethereal electric-blue glow benevolently radiating from number pad.

He spoke into creation's perfection, but she could hear no words. Every sound in her world had evanesced into the background of oblivion. All her senses were equally incapacitated. Only a tunnel vision remained. Only a vision of cell phone.

Its exterior was simple and stunning. All black in color, the rectangular entity was the exact four-inch replica of the omniscient monolith from the movie *2001: A Space Odyssey*. Except the monolith from *2001* never had an incandescent blue number pad. Or protuberant video-game joystick that retracted when not erect.

He gracefully entered the establishment and took a seat across from her at the bar, still whispering sweet nothings into the phone, unable to break his worship of the mini-monolith, neatly reenacting the prehuman apes' behavior in *2001*.

She waited patiently. Finally he ended his sweet intercourse and caringly deposited the phone in the inner pocket of his sports coat, where it would rest by his heart.

She made her move. Kismet insisted upon it. Getting up from her seat, she sauntered up to him at the bar.

"Hello, you," she cooed to her stranger.

"Why, hello to you," he sheepishly smiled.

"You know," she sultrily revealed to him, "you had me at Nokia Ringtone #4."

"The cause of death is sudden cardiac arrest," stated the coroner, examining her body.

"Strange for a woman so young," said the investigating police officer while eyeing her lifeless form on the slab. "Are there any signs of criminality?"

"Not that I can detect so far," the coroner informed, continuing the autopsy.

"She's got a clean record. Thirty-year-old single white female. Affluent. Well-educated. High-paying job. Highly respected among her peers," said the cop.

"No record of drug use?" inquired the coroner.

"No, nothing. Although the guy from the bar she went home with says the first thing she did when they got back to his place was tell him she needed to use his cell phone. He says she ran into the bathroom as soon as he gave it to her."

"You think she needed to make a private little call to her dealer?" asked the medical examiner.

"I don't know. Sounds like that, but she doesn't fit the bill of a junkie," surmised the cop. "The guy says he waited a half hour for her to leave his bathroom. She didn't. He knocked on the door to see if she was OK. When there wasn't any answer, he went in to find her dead on the toilet. He says there was absolutely no physical or sexual contact between them, and his roommate, who was there, backs up his story."

"Well, there are no outward signs of physical trauma,"

assessed the coroner. "Wait a minute…oh, my God—" he stammered, inspecting her vagina. And then it came. And there it was.

Pulled out from her woman's prerogative: four inches of manly monolith; with retractable video-game joystick fully erect.

"Not another one of these," cringed the cop.

"Yes. The moistness of her vaginal cavity shorted out the cell phone's battery causing a sudden electric shock that stopped her heart," the coroner ruled. "At least Roxanne Pulitzer had the good sense to use a non-electric trumpet."

"This is becoming all too common," lamented the cop. "Just last Tuesday we bagged a woman who asphyxiated while fellating the tailpipe of a Porsche."

"Damn it!" sermonized the medical man. "There ought to be some sort of public information campaign for these people who put their lives at risk by cutting out the middleman and sleeping directly with the source of their affection!"

Thus, in order to prevent further tragedies, a warning from the surgeon general stating that cutting out the middleman and sleeping directly with the electrical and/or mechanical source of one's affection can be hazardous to a consumer's health is now posted on all caffeinated low-carb malt liquor beverages.

I retract it all. The cop never told that despicable story. Because that would require of him imagination. And a sense of humor that is a highly evolved, evolutionary dead end. You magisterially self-important species of narrow-minded priggish devolving chimps, you.

So instead the cop masturbated to pictures of burning napalm. Because he's a typical cop.

Jealous?

So the cop tries to douse me in napalm while masturbating. Because he's a typical cop. So I bugger off before he can bugger me while thinking about napalm.

There's range work to be done so the Mexicans are rounded up and driven. Because this is Arizona. The Mexicans are driven back to Mexico or New Mexico. Because no difference is understood. Because this is Arizona.

During the confusion of the melee I'm able to stupefy some averagely addled yuppies even more than previously stupefied. They're on the perfectly bourgeois quest for the Holy Grail which they and the other yuppies believe can be found and purchased from one of the many bygone-era curiosity and curiosa shops along Route 66. True believers that I am the latest accoutrement needing acquiring, they pile me in the Range Rover and we're off to the next purchasable accoutrement.

A pilgrimage that would take the yuppies from the yuppie mecca of Los Angeles to the yuppie mecca of Santa Fe.

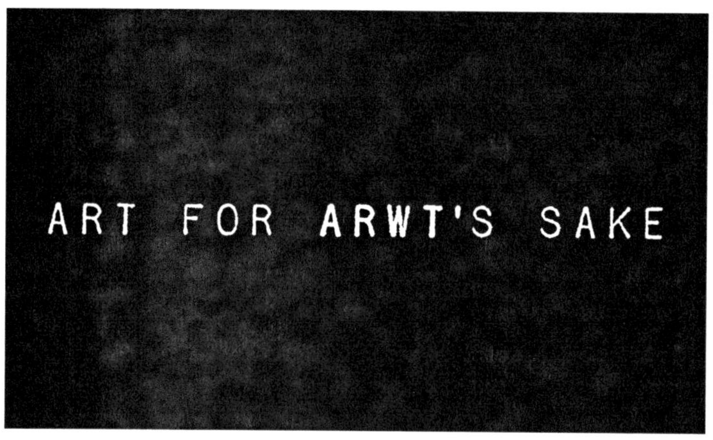

ART FOR ARWT'S SAKE

"It's a piece that speaks of the grand, empty spectatorship that modern-day life has become. It vividly portrays the association between our intensified pace of living with our avarice for, and worship of, novelties—and the distorted sense of reality that follows suit," says the toy Range Rover.

"How wonderful!" excitedly nods the yuppie twat flower as she stares vacuously at the painting.

"Oh, yes. I know all about that. You're saying it's art for art's sake," astutely observes yuppie twat flower's male counterpart (as photographed in *Bon Appétit, You Edacious Modern Swine*—a Condé Nast jewel). "May we have a moment to discuss it?"

"Why, of course. Call on me if you need any assistance," answers the miniature car at our feet before driving off to another part of the showroom.

He looks studiously at the work of art. Hand fondles chin in obvious deep reflection. With one eyebrow successfully cocked, he nods to himself, indicating the subtler nuances of the piece are certainly not lost on him. He follows with a slight scoff and chuckle, affirming he knows all too well the mindset of the artist in question and where the so-called creative soul had erred, albeit a small misstep. He then glances around the gallery to see who had noticed his acute discernment of all things fine.

She concludes: "It's *very good.* Just look at how expensive it is."

"Hmmm," he concurs.

My hand would fondle chin in deep reflection on which one of these modern flecks of turd I'm gonna start humping the leg of, if I had a hand.

She: "It's sending a potent environmental message; with all the vibrant greens splattered all over it."

After enough time passes to convince anyone watching that more contemplation had been achieved, he adds: "Ah, yes."

She: "The streaks of paint seem to leap off the canvas. So full of life. It has very deep meaning."

He: "Ah, it certainly does!" And it certainly does. The car had told them so.

"Well, I agree with everyone. This *is* the *hottest* gallery in Santa Fe!" she pronounces.

"Yes, it's well deserved. The pieces here are of exceptional quality. Fine examples of what modern art *should* be. Take this one for example,"—pointing at that painting that looks like all the rest—"an amateur would crudely dismiss this as the random spattering of a very bright green paint, whereas I have deduced the meaning of it, which is obvious, yet audacious."

"I see," his wife sees. "What do you see?"

"Of course," he concludes.

"Oh, yes," she replies.

I lick my asshole.

"It gels swimmingly with the entire theme of this splendid gallery. Take the sheer concrete walls of the building itself—"

"Oh, how wonderful."

"Yes. Simplicity. Four concrete walls within which this art is exhibited. Genius. No other rooms. No windows. Just four concrete walls and paintings. Marvelous."

"I see."

"And no human employees. The only humans present being

the patrons of the arts, who are left alone to wander, explore, admire, and grow. Ruthlessly efficient, mind you."

"Oh, how wonderful!"

"The only employee being a *car!* A miniature Range Rover that assists the patrons, answers their questions, and completes the bills of sale! Ingenious!"

"Oh, it is! And it's dog friendly!"

"Naturally. A statement on man's awakening to the need to embrace wildlife. This entire establishment stands in salute to man's *progress.* A vigorous testament to the blooming of humanity's innovation and insight. Yet it also retains that rebellious spirit of indignation that the best of art of the modern period reproduces time and time again. Indeed, the spartan concrete walls of the gallery are indicative of this, and the philosophy which I have just elucidated."

"I had a class on that in college."

"Indeed, as I just explained."

"It's no wonder all our friends are buying pieces from this gallery."

"Yes, we might have to acquire two or three. The clientele here is strictly top-notch."

Then, synchronicity: The front door of the concrete bunker bursts open, bringing a stop to the various patrons' whispered conversations of underling-class besmirchment. All eyes focus on the door suspended agape by not any physical implement but by the sheer aura of what awaits on the opposite end. The dry-ice rolling fog (with accompanying coruscating pyrotechnics) comes off without a hitch. And then: the man.

An exquisite masterpiece. A stately gentleman in his mid-forties with a fine salt-and-pepper crest of hair and a finer still collection of facial features. This handsome showpiece is patrician personified, with all necessary papers to prove it. The necessary accoutrements are also present: tuxedo, top hat, cane, Rolex watch with diamond-encrusted nuclear generator, scarf made from the silkiest of Sherpa hair (caught in the wild, not factory farmed), bulletproof monocle. He also enjoys the privilege of a third leg.

Naturally.

Stemming from tuxedo pants, where once a crotch had roamed, extends a third leg. To describe his walk as stately would not do him justice, for he does not merely sashay as he does gallop.

"The only truly sentient beings are those who can lick their own cocks!" I bark with a mouthful of cock (my own; see above).

The dozen well-bred gallery-goers are spellbound; and not by my cocksucking artistry. So goes my life: pearls before swine (see this book's reviews).

The dozen well-bred gallery-goers stare submissively at their liege. It is not often they find themselves in the presence of someone obviously superior. There is *old* money here—and a third leg to boot. Get it? *Third leg to boot?* Ha!

I re-lick my asshole.

The lord trots to the middle of the showroom. He acknowledges none with the benefit of eye contact. Peering above his nouveau riche and hopelessly parvenu juniors, he quickly judges the artwork, snapping and pointing in rapid succession at four separate paintings. The toy Range Rover, having quietly driven to his side, says deferentially, "Excellent choices, as always, My Lord. They'll be delivered to you by day's end."

With absolutely no recognition of the car's obeisance or anyone else's, the man of utter and terrible refinement gallops away.

Just like that, the noble human stool is gone.

Not needing further invitation, Mr. Bourgeois decisively and dramatically snaps his fingers. "*Garçon!* I mean, *le car!*" he summons.

"Yes, sir. May I be of assistance?" answers the Range Rover, rolling to us.

"Yes, my good man, you may be of assistance. I need to inquire a bit more about this piece here. What is—"

"No no no!" inserts Mrs. Bourgeois. "Who was *he*?"

"Ah, you're interested in the count?"

"A count he is!" she-bourgeois orgasms in best Yoda impersonation.

Car informs: "He is Count Count of Hanselvania. This nobleman of the finest refinement has dozens of ornate, baroque, terribly tasteful estates around the globe, including one here in a more secluded spot of Santa Fe. It is called the *Brown Palace*—named after the help, apparently."

"*Oh!* How wonderful!" she-bourgeois femininely ejaculates.

The car continues: "An avid art collector with a genius's eye, Count Count has taken a certain fondness to our humble little gallery, and has been our most benevolent, generous patron. Indeed, the special affinity between Count Count and the ARWT Gallery has allowed for this to grow into the longest-lived relationship we have had the pleasure of knowing in our rather short, yet phenomenally successful, stint in selling art."

"*Oh!* How wonderful!"

"It is. Count Count is the finest of gentlemen. Regal in every sense of the word. A sublime radiance truly shines from his core, showering those fortunate enough to be in his presence with uncommon illumination."

"Wonderful!"

"Yes. We have been very fortunate to have him as a patron this long."

"Such an elegant man. Such a worldly benefactor. Such a sage old soul—and I can always tell these things."

"I have no doubt, madam."

"Such a dynamic being. Such a profound persona. Such a marvelously *equipped* man."

"Ah, you have quite the discerning eye."

He-bourgeois groans.

She-bourgeois moans: "I'm certain a man so *well-endowed* with all the *finer things* must make his countess quite the happy lady."

"Well, madam, unfortunately Countess Count died only six months ago."

"*Oh!* How dreadful!" smiles she-bourgeois.

"I will be sure to pass along your condolences to the count, madam."

"Please do! The name is Mia Bourgeois, of Los Angeles."

"And I am *Doctor* Noah Bourgeois—ophthalmologist at large and *her husband*."

"Charmed to meet you. My name is Skolnik," the car's dignified human voice (oxymoron) announces.

She-Bourgeois: "Tell me more about Countess Count's death. *C'est tragique!*"

"Indeed. The countess was an enthusiastic sun worshipper. A bronzed goddess. She demanded all lighting in her palatial Brown Palace be upgraded with tanning bed bulbs. The hired help, being earthy swarthy migrant-labor folk, withstood the constant onslaught of UV rays. The count's top hat and bullet-proof monocle shielded him. But, alas, the fair-haired countess had no defense."

"How horrible!" squeals she-Bourgeois.

"Yes," agrees Skolnik. "It is said she was fondling one of her newly acquired paintings from our gallery when her skin snapped, crackled, and popped."

He-Bourgeois: "Good God!"

"Lupe the maid, and Lupe's feather duster, were within the fifty-foot blast range and went up in the inferno. Most tragically, so did the painting."

"The poor artwork!" lament the Bourgeoisie in unison.

"The feather duster is replaceable; as is obviously the maid;

the painting is sadly not," concludes Skolnik. "The coroner ruled it as another death via spontaneous human combustion—natural causes."

"Naturally," rules Dr. Bourgeois.

"Soon after the countess's passing, the count—in coping with his grief—took on his third leg."

"Naturally," rules Dr. Bourgeois. "He's suddenly single and playing the field. Might as well *accentuate* his positives!"

Car: "Ahem."

Dr. Bourgeois: "I work in the same exclusive L.A. hospital as Dr. Josef Elegnem—the penile implant doctor of the stars. He got me Ellen DeGeneres's autograph."

Car: "Have you any other questions?"

Dr. Bourgeois: "I have deduced that all of your pieces are by the same *artiste*."

"Yes, sir. The same artist has created all these pieces. His name is ARWT. That's why this place is named the ARWT Gallery."

She-Bourgeois: "A-R-W-T. What a lovely name! It's a name that says, 'I have the soul of an artist.' Like 'Art,' only more exotic!"

He-Bourgeois: "ARWT. The name sounds Scandinavian."

She-Bourgeois: "Oh, yes! Just like IKEA! I bet they're relatives!"

"My mother's side can trace their Aryan roots all the way back to Lothar the Beheader in 1431," he-Bourgeois gloats.

Skolnik salutes, "Well, then you'll appreciate the name ARWT, in all capital letters if you please, is the name of the ancient Norse god of gun repair."

"I *was* aware of that," reveals he-Bourgeois.

"What's his last name?" she asks.

Skolnik answers, "He has no last name, just one name—*ARWT*. Like *Cher*, only with less pubic hair."

"*Oh*, so exotic!" she gushes.

"Yes. I'd like to commend his natural artistry. So course, yet elegant. So natural, yet contrived. So alive, yet dead. So deadening, yet impacting," explains he-Bourgeois.

"Oh, most certainly! His paintings are all so vibrant! They seem to reek of him! His essence does nothing short of radiate from the canvas right into his captive audience. It's as if I feel ARWT penetrating me right now," she pants.

Skolnik: "The theme of these pieces, and the gallery itself, centers on the externalization of life in contemporary society. Modern technology, with its ability to instantaneously disseminate information through mass media, has enabled us to experience life more and more as a spectator. Contextless information that usually consists of partial truths, innuendoes, and banal trivialities is churned out at breakneck speed by the mass media. This incessant background noise of information becomes contemporary man's *now know-how*—a specious stand-in for true knowledge and insight. Under a constant barrage of pictures, sounds, text, and numbers, it comes to be almost impossible to differentiate the mass media rendition of life from the real thing, until most people forget there is such a difference."

"The modern world has come to consecrate *technique.* We are taught to celebrate technique's complete triumph; its domination of human society. But this is myopic hubris. For a world dominated by technique is a world that's come to be dominated by *externals.* Drowned out is the ability to reflect and the self-knowledge that stems from it which one needs in order to become an actual *individual,*" I bark between mouthfuls of cock.

Skolnik: "This art here revolts against these depersonalizing forces of present-day society and depicts the lonely, uncommon struggle to become a real individual living a real life in opposition to the great modern drive toward a homogenized mass society."

"Ah, yes. I heard that on NPR," informs Dr. Bourgeois.

I contemplate how best to rip out his jugular. Which I saw on PBS.

Skolnik: "As society becomes ever more specialized, the more it loses sight of any broader perspective. A professional man—which is what society breeds—such as an ophthalmologist, tends to see things from the frame of reference of his specialty, which his life revolves around, and loses count of whatever falls outside this narrow field. Yes, a specialized vision allows for a much sharper focus. But the narrower and more specialized our vision, the more the periphery—the larger picture—becomes impossible to see."

"Which is why good eye health is so important."

"Through this narrowed professional deformation, mad obsession with technology and its trinkets, and his own warped reasoning, man has become blind, fractured, alienated, detached. He has so reasoned everything, that paradoxically, the way he lives has become unreasonable. This entire gallery is a testament to man's detachment from his surroundings, and in the end, his detachment from what it is to be human."

"*Oh*, how wonderfully true!" applauds she-Bourgeois.

"This theme, this philosophy, permeates everything—from the art, right down to me, the miniature Range Rover. A toy car with a human's voice is the gallery's only apparent custodian. Is it real or just something seen secondhand on TV? Reality and someone else's rendering of it become blended.

"As in everyday life, here in this gallery you speak of trivialities all day long to a novelty item: a miniaturized version of a gaudy, wasteful, luxury automobile—a status symbol that so many place so great an importance, and yet, is it important? Are we truly that blind?"

"Agreed. You speak persuasively of the importance of a more farsighted energy policy," spits out Dr. Bourgeois' programmed programming.

"And in regard to the art pieces, one comes here armed only with contrived niceties and an imperious elitist demeanor in order to acquire material objects perceived to be valuable, but at day's end, *are* just objects. Then one will go back home to emptily display these objects to others of the same formidable vacuity, and back to work in order to trade some more life for monetary currency, which will be used to purchase more novelties, perhaps even more artwork from this gallery, never thinking about whether any of this pattern makes any sense, but having the good sense in knowing only that they can show, albeit for a short period before their death, a trifle of supposed great worth."

"The artwork here *is* of great worth," agrees he-Bourgeois.

"*Great* worth," regurgitates she-Bourgeois.

"We've been to *so* many *so-called* art galleries. But this one, as we heard, *is* different. Not so much different as in a break from the acceptable, but different as in *superior.* Your glowing write-up in *The New York Times* was certainly justified."

"You would just be shocked and appalled at the state of art nowadays," she-Bourgeois promises the Range Rover. "Any handyman with a paintbrush and a can of Sherwin Williams seems to think he can paint!"

"We have purchased various pieces from the hot galleries here in Santa Fe, and elsewhere. But this work here is *very* hot right now. You definitely deserve to be known as the moment's premier purveyor of art."

"Oh, it's just appalling the caliber—or lack thereof—of craft seen in many art galleries nowadays."

"Yes. Some of the brushwork in your neighbor's gallery is frightfully sloppy. Oh, I suppose they had passable craftsmanship. But I found it to be a little knavish, and certainly lacking of the artist's soul."

"*Oh*, it was disgraceful. The Masters would roll over in their graves to see such a perversion of the craft."

"It pleases me that you fine people seem intent on joining the sage few who appreciate—*and can afford*—ARWT's offerings," lauds the Range Rover. "Now, which one of our masterpieces shall you be acquiring today?"

Six months later a knock comes from the Bourgeoisie's front door.

"Answer the door!" I bark. "I'm busy licking my ginormous cock!"

She-Bourgeois peeks through the peephole viewer. "May I help you?" she calls suspiciously through the door.

"Yes, madam. My name is Skolnik. I'm from the ARWT Gallery." Same voice as the one that came from the toy Range Rover.

She opens the door. "Why, hello there! What a pleasant surprise!"

"Yes, Mrs. Bourgeois. The pleasure is mine," announces a man in his early fifties.

"What a marvelous suit you're wearing. Please excuse *my* appearance. I wasn't expecting company. I'm afraid the help has the day off, but would you still care to come in?"

"Yes, thank you," Skolnik says, entering.

It's a standardized abode built to impress standardized aficionados. The interior boasts some modish motif, furniture made of former old-growth forest residents, and other multifarious unsustainably and therefore conventionally produced bauble comprising the mandated trappings of modern success.

"What a lovely home you have, Mrs. Bourgeois," smiles Skolnik.

"Why, thank you."

"A fine placement for a fine piece," he comments, pointing at one of the ARWT Gallery's paintings hanging prominently in the foyer.

"Why, yes! I'm glad you approve. Such a wonderful piece. Everyone we've shown it to says so."

I roll over onto my back to show them my wonderful piece.

"I think you'll also love what we've done with the sitting room," she tells him. "This way, please."

"It's wonderful," confirms Skolnik upon sight of the second painting hanging above the Italian leather whatever.

Properly seated under the chef-d'oeuvre's spectacular effulgence, the genial hostess inquires of guest: "Mr. Skolnik, what brings you to Los Angeles all the way from Santa Fe?"

"Well, Mrs. Bourgeois, we at the ARWT Gallery always take an active interest in our clients. It's policy to occasionally drop in on our various friends to see how they're doing with their art. These intimate bonds that we seek to create through material objects—our art—constitute a paradoxical dichotomy."

"Naturally," nods Mrs. Bourgeois.

"The paradox being that we attempt to generate real feeling in our relationships with our buyers—love, fear, hate, joy, arousal, anguish. These are the *real* things that comprise true living which is perpetually being supplanted in the modern world by material decoys. But while we attempt to pullulate these very real, very human feelings, we also never lose sight of the irony that our art, which is designed to bring forth all those emotions that comprise the true human spirit, is just a material object itself taking as its subject the depersonalized detachment endemic in our society."

"Can I get you something to drink?"

"No, thank you. Is your husband at home?"

"No. He's at the hospital today."

"I see. His eye work keeps him preoccupied and away."

"It's his life."

"I regret I wasn't able to see him on this calling. Has he been as satisfied with the artwork as you've apparently been?"

"He loves them. His fellow ophthalmologists were all envious when he told them how valuable the works are."

"And is the third piece you purchased in an equally prominent location as the two I've already seen?"

"*Oh*, yes. It's upstairs in the nursery. I mean, the study. It would have been—" the remainder of the sentence trailing off in a muddle of tears.

"Mrs. Bourgeois, I'm sorry, are you all right?" Skolnik asks with genuine compassion.

"Oh, yes. I'm sorry. I should certainly be over it by now. We were expecting a baby in November, but I miscarried her last month," she slurs in between hiccups of grief.

"I am *so* sorry," laments Skolnik. "I know this must be a terrible and difficult time for you. But things like angst, fear, despair, and death are all part of what it is to be human. We not only forget this, but we try to subvert it from reality; tranquilize it from existence. But that never works, and we continue to grow even more forlorn, angry, and impotent."

"*Oh*, yes," she agrees, popping a tranquilizer into her mouth. "*Doctor's orders!*"

"I'm afraid it's time for me to take my leave."

"I do wish you could have stayed longer," she says, escorting him to the door.

"Please pass along my regards to Dr. Bourgeois."

"It looks like you can do it yourself. Here comes Noah now," she says as hubby hobbles from his life-sized Range Rover up the driveway. "Noah! This gentleman is Mr. Skolnik. You know, the car voice from the ARWT Gallery?"

"Ah, yes, of course! Pleased to meet you again," says Dr.

Bourgeois, shaking Skolnik's huge gloved hand. "And may I say, that's a fabulous suit you have on!"

"Thank you so much. My tailor will be pleased to hear of your kind compliments," says Skolnik.

"Who is your tailor?" he asks.

"This suit was generously provided by the American Radioactive Waste Treasury. All of it: the industrial-strength rip-proof gloves, the fully enclosed lead-plated bodysuit, the self-contained oxygen respirator," wheezes Skolnik through his space helmet.

"*Oh*, how wonderful!" exclaims Mrs. Bourgeois.

"Indeed," seconds Dr. Bourgeois.

"It's all in keeping with the ARWT Gallery's philosophy on man's detachment from man, as we've discussed."

"I believe I've heard of the American Radioactive Waste Treasury," says Dr. Bourgeois.

"Probably. Besides supplying our humble little ARWT Gallery with the proper attire, they also concoct new and exciting ways of storing nuclear waste."

"Ah, yes. I read the article in *The New York Times*."

"It doesn't surprise me that a man with as much now know-how as yourself is familiar with the American Radioactive Waste Treasury. They're always focusing an eye on your future."

"Ha!" I bark! "Speaking of!"

"My colleagues at the hospital can't make heads or tails of this—" Dr. Bourgeois' third eye winks open in his forehead. "Just popped up over night—much like the third arm that's budding out of my chest."

"*Oh!* It's such a shame it couldn't be a third leg," regrets wife.

They watch as Skolnik walks down the sidewalk to the art appraisal/hazmat team. Dr. Bourgeois waves goodbye. In another six months he'll be able to wave while juggling.

And behind the modern-thinking couple, the painting in the foyer entitled *Gray Is All Theory, Green Is Life's Glowing Tree* glows an incandescent green. And would for the next twenty-four thousand years—guaranteed.

And Skolnik voices over: "For every one individual who repines that man has the intelligence to create wondrous technologies but not the wisdom to use them—or *not* use them—there are a million more who applaud that it's art for ARWT's sake."

I lick my fifth leg.

Having enough Snausages in your system will block the deleterious effects of massive amounts of radiation with the Snausages' own deleterious effects. Remember this when becoming a laughable survivalist freak planning your doomsday bomb shelter 'n kiddie-porn dungeon. Because hoarding Snausages for an Armageddon soiree like a good American is more sensible than insisting that America take real leadership in ridding the world of nuclear weapons that probability states will eventually be exploded because given a long enough timeline and unknowable events it's unreasonable to assume a society's nuclear weapons eventually *won't* be exploded.

Human history is the history of societies being born and built, only to decline and die so that other societies may be born to take their place. (After all, there aren't any Sumerians running around anymore because if there were, America would have killed them for their oil and ziggurats. I mean, to free them.) But a nuclear-armed society does not allow for this natural societal life cycle of death and rebirth to continue. A nuclear-armed society in its death throes will make sure that *nothing* lives past it. That is arrogant, insane, and by any meaningful definition, evil.

America is the only country powerful enough to impress upon the rest of the world that nuclear weapons are the enemy of all life. If the unacceptable threat of nuclear weapons is to ever be extinguished, if the presence of nuclear weapons is to ever be called what it really is—the worst of all crimes—then America must lead the way. America, the superpower, is the only country with the power to compel *all* nations of the world to dispel the omnicidal anathema of nuclear weapons.

But America won't. Because America would have to give up its own nuclear weapons. And America won't. Because America is America.

Or maybe it's just something inherent in you humans. Destined from the start to destroy yourselves. And take all other complex life with you. Not that you give a shit about the others (*humanity is and always has been paramount!* whispers your whore of a Mother Culture). Fuck it. Keep fellating yourselves at your Optimist Club gangbangs and hope your technology will end up only completely enslaving you as opposed to leaving you crispy around the edges.

So I leave the intellectual desert of Los Angeles for the next-door desert of Mojave in order to build my underground kiddie-porn shelter.

Jealous?

It takes a few days to complete the trip from sprawl to sand. I make good time hoofing it. I've always been fast. With a fifth leg I'm Tom Jones-fast. Depending on wind speed.

Four legs good, two legs bad, five legs badass!

While in the middle of the desert you meet the darndest miscreants. Like Moses.

Born in the fourteenth century B.C. in suburban Egypt, Moses never intended to become God's bringer of holy deliverance and boil-spurting death. His real love was interior decorating. But a glut of feng shuists on the Egyptian job market forced him into the Hebrew liberator/lawgiver/prophet racket.

Here now, the interview (as printed in last month's *Vainglorious Steaming Pile Printed for the Specious-*

Intellectualism Demographic Chock-Full o' Trivialities Posing as Important Topics Such as Interviews with Individuals with the Veneer of Interestingness Because You're So Not Individual or Interesting magazine—a Condé Nast jewel).

GUANO: You look great for being thirty-three hundred years old.
MOSES: This isn't natural. I've got Botox and plastic all the way down to my wooden staff.
GUANO: And that's not at all in a gay way.
MOSES: All faggots burn in hell. *Praise Yahweh!*
GUANO: What are Moses' hobbies and interests?
MOSES: Anything cockfighting.
GUANO: Speaking of, let's chat about your involvement in the ten plagues of Egypt.
MOSES: Ah, sweet memories.
GUANO: These were desperate times for your Israelites. According to the press release.
MOSES: It was horrific. Pharaoh of Egypt was hoarding all of the land's product.
GUANO: Product?
MOSES: Hair care product.
GUANO: Were there other privations?
MOSES: Pharaoh also hoarded the fun clothes. The shendyt kilts, the nemes headdresses, Prada loafers. I was left with pleather sandals and a rayon robe not even Hugh Heffner would wear. Thankfully I've burned most of the photos. And then *He* came to me.
GUANO: *He?*
MOSES: God. I can still see Him now—trying to hide behind that bush He lit on fire. Silly bitch singed His eyebrows doing it.
GUANO: Did you actually see God's face?
MOSES: Sure sure.

GUANO: What does God look like?

MOSES: Janet Reno.

God

GUANO: But according to Exodus 33:20, God says: *"Thou canst not see my face; for man shall not see Me and live."*

MOSES: Well, a little part of me did die that day. He looks like Janet Reno for God's sake.

GUANO: What did God want?

MOSES: He was just really pissy.

GUANO: At what?

MOSES: Pharaoh.

GUANO: God didn't like seeing his people in bondage?

MOSES: No. I have photographs proving He's *very* into bondage.

GUANO: Say, they'd look pretty good on the wall of my bomb shelter dungeon thingy.

MOSES: Whichever supranational corporate media steaming pile cums all over my face with the biggest gob of cash can print 'em.

GUANO: That's a Condé Nast jewel.

MOSES: It turns out I wasn't the only one pissed over the lack of clothes shopping. God was furious about being forced to dress like a Seventh-day Adventist.

GUANO: And the lack of product never helps a vengeful God's disposition.

MOSES: Yeah. You've seen what Janet Reno's hair looks like.

GUANO: What did He want you to do about it?

MOSES: Kill 'em all. He is God after all.

GUANO: Naturally.

MOSES: So my bro Aaron and I commandeered some drums of industrial waste stored in low-income neighborhoods—because some things never change—and dumped the contents into the Nile.

GUANO: I'm familiar with radioactive waste.

MOSES: It was far worse than radioactive waste.

GUANO: It was Snausages?

MOSES: Manischewitz wine.

GUANO: Obviously that would kill everything in the river.

MOSES: I also dumped in that God-awful robe. The friction from synthetic fibers striking the "wine" caught the river on fire for an hour.

GUANO: Exodus 7:18-19: *"And the fish that is in the river shall die, and the river shall stink; and the Egyptians shall lothe to drink of the water of the river. And the Lord spake unto Moses, Say unto Aaron, Take thy rod, and stretch out thine hand upon the waters of Egypt, upon their streams, upon their rivers, and* *upon their ponds, and upon all their pools of water, that they may become blood; and that there may be blood throughout all the land of Egypt...*"

MOSES: 'Twas Manischewitz. They wished it was blood.

GUANO: I'm just telling you what Exodus says.

MOSES: That is the first time ever the Bible has been misinterpreted or proved to be wrong.

GUANO: So the Manischewitz killed most everything in the river.

MOSES: Let's say the only thing that could live in it was a particularly nasty strain of algae named *Pfiesteria*. It proceeded to bloom in the waterways of Egypt. *Pfiesteria* makes a suite of toxins that narcotized and killed any fish unlikely enough to have survived my lil' stunt. The algae actually dissolved their still-living flesh—like a lawyer. The leaking blood of the dying fish, along with the red tinge from that particular strain of algae, will fashionably complement Manischewitz when trying this at home.

GUANO: What happened next?

MOSES: Pharaoh still wouldn't budge. No product or halter tops.

GUANO: Time for plague number two. Exodus 8:1-3: "*And the Lord spake unto Moses, Go unto Pharaoh, and say unto him, Thus saith the Lord, Let my people go, that they may serve me.*"

MOSES: Oh yes. With Him it's always about *Him*.

GUANO: "*And if thou [Pharaoh] refuse to let them go, behold, I will smite all thy borders with frogs: And the river shall bring forth frogs abundantly, which shall go up and come into thine house, and into thy bedchamber, and upon thy bed, and into the house of thy servants, and upon thy people, and into thine ovens, and into thy kneadingtroughs.*"

MOSES: The Nile was polluted. It was undrinkable. Nothing could live there. The fish couldn't get out; they died. The frogs could get out; they jumped onto the land. Right into the

Egyptians' tract homes.

GUANO: I'd buy that for a dollar.

MOSES: Everything was thrown out of balance. With the fish all dead, and nothing to feed on the frog eggs, huge numbers of little amphibians hatched, and then fled the toxic river for land.

GUANO: Only they weren't frogs. They were toads.

MOSES: In the Bible there's only one word for frogs and toads: *tsephardea*. The chiselers who wrote the Bible knew that anyone who believed what they'd written would be incapable of understanding. Anything. This includes: a) that the Bible was written as a practical joke by the Knights Templar in order to b) receive facials full of gobs of cash from supranational corporate media steaming piles which would c) facilitate future generations of chiselers in bilking future generations of dullards, oh, and d) that frogs and toads were two different creatures. So they lumped them under one word: tsephardea. During the Bible's transcription the learned scholars translated tsephardea to mean frog when it really meant toad. Lots of toads.

GUANO: This is only the second time ever the Bible has been misinterpreted or proved to be wrong.

MOSES: Frogs have the decency not to blight the world by reproducing in disgustingly vulgar numbers. Toads have the huge clutches of eggs necessary to multiply obscenely—like humans. Toads are attracted to heat and light sources because that's where the bugs they eat usually are.

GUANO: Thus the behavior of coming up onto the land and getting into the bread and going into ovens.

MOSES: Just like Jews.

GUANO: So the toads choked the land and then started dying. Exodus 8:13-14: *"[T]he frogs died out of the houses, out of the villages, and out of the fields. And they gathered them together upon heaps: and the land stank."*

MOSES: Yes. They all *croaked*.

GUANO: Ha!
MOSES: Pun-umental!
GUANO: What killed them?
MOSES: Either the lack of water due to the polluted river or the lack of product.
GUANO: Or the puns.
MOSES: Pun-licious!
GUANO: Speaking of plagues, plague number three. Exodus 8:17: "*...Aaron stretched out his hand with his rod, and smote the dust of the earth, and it became lice in man, and in beast; all the dust of the land became lice throughout all the land of Egypt...so there were lice upon man, and upon beast.*"
MOSES: It wasn't lice. Lice that attack humans do not attack animals.
GUANO: This is only the third time ever the Bible has been misinterpreted or proved to be wrong.
MOSES: You'll have to forgive the Knights Templar for the mistake. They were so chewed up by syphilis from their cock-sucking grandmothers they couldn't tell biting lice from their grandmothers' teeth.
GUANO: What insect was it?
MOSES: The midge. You may also call it a gnat. Or a *no-see-um* if you possess a bonus forty-seventh chromosome.
GUANO: Then plague number four. Exodus 8:24: "*[There came a grievous swarm of flies into the house of Pharaoh, and into his servants' houses, and into all the land of Egypt: the land was corrupted by reason of the swarm of flies.*"
MOSES: The flies were a literary metaphor for Las Vegas tourists.
GUANO: Obviously an insult to flies.
MOSES: The population of stable flies boomed because there were no predators (i.e., toads) to keep them in check.
GUANO: Plague number five, courtesy of Exodus 9:3: "*Behold, the hand of the Lord is upon thy cattle which is in the field, upon*

the horses, upon the asses—"
MOSES: *Oh*, His hand was always upon the asses.
GUANO: *"—upon the camels, upon the oxen, and upon the sheep: there shall be a very grievous murrain."*
MOSES: So the wall-to-wall insect infestation starts spreading disease. Could've been African horse sickness—a virus which affects horses, mules, asses. A nifty little bug that grows in the cells that line the blood vessels throughout the host animal's body. The cells deteriorate rapidly. Blood winds up in the lungs and the animal drowns in its own body fluid. The entire process can kill within hours. And African horse sickness has a close relative—Bluetongue—which kills cattle, sheep, and goats. Both of these similar diseases are spread by the same insect: the biting midge.
GUANO: Environmental changes (the polluting of the river) started a chain of events propagating an insect explosion which led to a plague. But how did you prevent this disease from affecting your own people's animals?
MOSES: The Israelites and their comparatively better-smelling livestock were safe from the midges which are weak fliers. With a range of fifty yards, the midges couldn't reach the Israelites who were partitioned off from the Egyptian section of town. You know those Jews and their ghettos.
GUANO: Plague number six: boils and blains. Huzzah!
MOSES: Caused by glanders, a bacterial infection. It affects both animals and humans, causing their lymph nodes to swell and separate, hence the whimsical name. It often leads to death.
GUANO: And spread by the stable fly.
MOSES: Yes. But that's not all! Exodus 9:10: *"And they took ashes of the furnace, and stood before Pharaoh; and Moses sprinkled it up toward heaven; and it became a boil breaking forth with blains upon man, and upon beast."* Did I mention that glanders was used as a biological warfare agent in the First

and Second World Wars?

GUANO: Huzzah! Moses was the world's first bioterrorist!

MOSES: Well, it was easy enough to cook some shit up using Reuben and Issachar's meth manger.

GUANO: You should sue those injured or killed in any glanders biological attack during the First and Second World Wars for copyright infringement.

MOSES: I know my rights under the System's perverse "justice" system. I'm a Jew; and a lawyer (redundant).

GUANO: Whether the glanders was spread via the booming stable fly infestation or Moses, what prevented the disease from spreading to the Israelites?

MOSES: The range of the stable fly is only one mile, again sparing the Israelites. And any bioterror weapon released onto the public would be negated by gas masks owned by every good paranoid Israeli.

GUANO: Interviews with individuals with the veneer of interestingness do not qualify as credible steaming piles of corporate journalism unless there's a gotcha question, for ratings' sake. It says in Exodus 3:21-22 that before the onset of the plagues, God says to you: *"I will give [your] people favor in the sight of the Egyptians, and it will happen that when you go, you shall not go empty-handed. But every woman shall ask of [the Egyptians]...jewels of silver, jewels of gold, and clothing; and you shall put them on your sons, and on your daughters. You shall despoil the Egyptians."*

MOSES: Sure sure. Rob them and kill them. *Now that's religion!* Or nationalism. Or communism. Or capitalism. Or fascism. Or technologization (the modern world's true ideology). Oppression, torture, enslavement, murder in the name of any thought-terminating ideology is a time-honored human tradition.

GUANO: I'd buy that for a dollar. On to plague number seven. Exodus 9:22: *"And the Lord said unto Moses, Stretch forth thine* *hand toward heaven, that there may be hail in all the land of Egypt, upon man, and upon beast, and upon every herb of the field."*

MOSES: Hail is not unusual in the region. With the death of the fish and the sickness of the Egyptians' livestock, the bludgeoning of their crops by hail further reduced their protein sources. This caused great distress since they were all on trendy low-carb diets.

GUANO: Plague number eight treats the Egyptians to locusts.

MOSES: Swarms of locusts have never been uncommon. They'd go searching for any remaining crops undamaged by the hail. And their numbers may have increased because of the lack of predators, like toads. Which exacerbated the food shortage and sickness.

GUANO: Plague number nine. Exodus 10:22-23: *"[A]nd there was a thick darkness in all the land of Egypt three days: they saw not one another, neither rose any from his place for three days..."*

MOSES: Yeah. As the Jesuits like to say: what the fuck?

GUANO: A volcanic eruption that spewed ash? Or a powerful sandstorm? They occasionally ravage the region. A solar eclipse? Swarms of locusts blocking out the sun?

MOSES: No. Lacking the courage and free minds to critically analyze the malignant existence they had created for themselves, the Egyptians instead retreated into a virtual reality "existence" of Facebook, Twitter, Xboxes, iPhones, iPads, eSmegma, etc.

GUANO: Sure beats livin'. Which brings us to the bestest plague ever! Number ten: God goes off and kills the Egyptians' firstborn!

MOSES: The scientific explanation: Hail and locusts decimate the Egyptians' crops. Hail is wet. Locusts shit. Anything edible remaining in the fields is picked hastily while still damp and shitty and put into small storerooms under the desert sands where they rot while the Egyptians are rotting in their houses for three days electronically masturbating. Mold grows on the moist, soiled seed and produces deadly mycotoxins. Under famine conditions the eldest sons customarily receive the most food and thus eat the most toxins and thus die. Which led to "Undeciphered Cryptic B," my op-ed piece in the Dead Sea Scrolls in which I learnedly rant on the need to destroy your house if mildew appears. Unless you're a landlord—in which case throw up some wallpaper over the shit so your tenants can't see it and bitch.

GUANO: Like in that classic *Home Improvement* rerun starring Tim Allen!

MOSES: Yes. But I'm not suing Tim Allen for copyright infringement. I'm just having him disemboweled with his entrails stuffed in his mouth.

GUANO: Which is something we can all get behind.

MOSES: The Israelites ate lamb, herbs, and unleavened bread—the ceremonial Passover items that would have been safe from the mold contamination that killed the Egyptians.

GUANO: And they had the good sense to streak their doors with lambs' blood.

MOSES: They most certainly did not. Putting blood on the door is too tacky even for a Jew. However here's another home improvement tip: If you streak your door with Manischewitz, God will never visit you. The Everliving is scared shitless of it.

GUANO: In the end you killed ten percent of the Egyptian population.

MOSES: Yeah. Mostly kids. Remember: If you wind up on the winning side, conventional history will always frame it up as "a struggle for freedom" or some other inflated rose-scented steaming pile the brainwashed masses get to regurgitate to each other on holidays.

GUANO: Well, one man's terrorist is another dolt's Bible icon. Or heroic patriot. Or inflated rose-scented steaming pile fellated by the brainwashed masses.

MOSES: Take it from Moses: Better to be fellated by the idiot masses than labeled "terrorist" and having AC Delco jumpstart your testicles in America's secret worldwide torture prisons.

GUANO: Because modern society in its monolithic, maniacal drive for ever greater technological progress certainly doesn't on a daily basis commit millions of the most heinous acts of terrorism against both humanity and the planet.

MOSES: That's an idea which requires actual broad vision which requires a free mind which requires a mind practiced in critical thinking. (I.e., not commercially viable.) Far easier to throw any dreg unwise enough to impede society's progress in the process of centralization into America's worldwide torture prisons.

GUANO: After all, modern readers don't buy vainglorious steaming piles printed for the specious-intellectualism demographic chock-full o' trivialities posing as important topics in order to challenge their own oh-so thoroughly inculcated and entrenched Weltanschauung.

MOSES: Or: just keep throwing up some wallpaper over the shit so the tenants can't see it and bitch.

Then Hellevator pops up through the desert floor and spits out *The New Yorker*. And fireballs and spittle. IN 3-D! A Condé Nast jewel.

HELLAVATOR 2: ELECTRIC BOOGALOO

Ding!

Hellevator! leaps and snorts and opens its doors and grabs Moses with its forked tongue (in director's cut only). I step forward (heroically). "Everyone, take shelter under my GINORMOUS cock!" I bark! Realizing there is no television crew chronicling the heroic line I withdraw to my dressing room to lick my asshole.

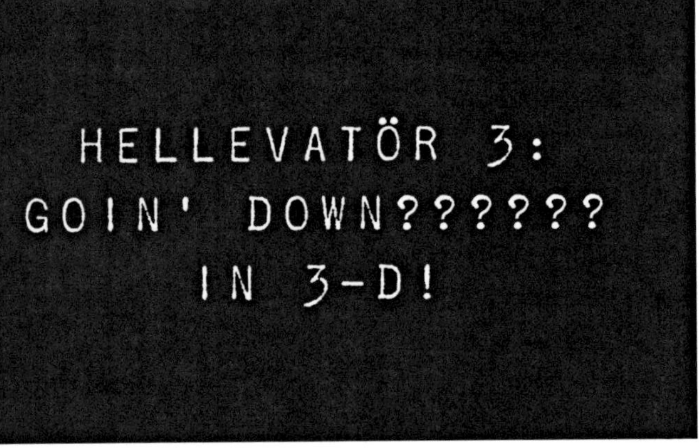

Ding!

Hellevator! pops out of the dressing room floor and tickles me with forked tongue. You know, foreplay. "With a tongue like that we must form our own gang and get a reality show," I bark!

I unsheathe my ginormous cock which is a turgid golden fire hose which speeds straight out at the audience in 3-D. The scene is serene and softly suspended.

Insert video of me dueling Hellevator with my ginormous cock (heroically) here.

Hellevator leaps and snorts and ejaculates gobs of corporate mass media cash all over my face. The scene is serene and softly suspended.

The End??????????

ISLAND

Hellevator pops out of a beach made of garbage and drops me off. "Shit. I'm back in L.A."

"Now that the oceans and ocean life are loaded with pollutants like cadmium, aluminum, chromium, lead, silver, mercury, titanium, along with oil, sewage, fertilizers, solid garbage, and a wide selection of toxic chemicals, you're better off out of the water and on a beach made of filth," Moses consoles.

One of the natives eats a fish fresh from the ocean and drops dead.

"Our worries will be over once the U.S. Department of Agriculture makes Heavy Metals the fifth food group," I bark!

Then the USDA makes Heavy Metals the fifth food group. Sponsored by The Man!santo. Et al.

Moses says: "While we are knee-deep in litter, we aren't knee-deep in humans with breast, biceps, triceps, cheek, chin, jaw, lip, buttocks, calf, and penile implants; face, arm, bra-line back, thigh, and whole-body lifts; liposuction, Botox, conforming labia mutilation; all, all with modish tattoos to prove how fearlessly individualistic they are. So we're not in L.A."

A native child wanders up to me so naturally I have to decide whether to bite its head. I choose not to and make a mistake. "Hi there, little boy. You'd look great in my kiddie-porn dungeon."

Moses is concerned. So he asks the boy: "Shouldn't you be indoors playing with yourself and video games while texting while shoving a Ritalin suppository in the one orifice you're not shoving mass-produced heavily processed genetically modified Corn'ums while working on a modern weight problem?"

"But I'm not fat," says the sinewy barechested boy in hemp shorts as he drops into a handstand and proceeds to walk on his palms in a youthful explosion of physicalness.

"Don't be so defensive, tubby," I bark! "Remember: Modern humans aren't supposed to move that way unless it's required by their field of specialization."

The boy cartwheels down the beach and backflips onto a black stallion. A horse, even.

"Snot-nosed showoff. Let's go bite his head."

"Wait. This must be the part of the book which shows a just and decent society producing humans that are happy, whole, self-actualized individuals. It's a very short and fictional chapter," assures Moses.

"I am Huxley," announces the boy atop the stallion. "Welcome to the island of Pala. You are the first visitors we've ever had."

"That's only because you're not properly marketing yourselves. An entire beach made of garbage is very popular with the modern sluggard leisurely wallowing in their own filth demographic. See Los Angeles. Especially if you're a modern sluggard who enjoys long moonlit walks on the beach made of their own filth," I bark!

"I wasn't aware anybody from the outside world knew we were here," Huxley says.

"That's because you have a marketing problem. Pay attention or I'll break out the Ritalin blowdart. Which makes medicating the kids fun again!" I bark! "I will help you market your trash beach to the world as soon as you ejaculate gobs of cash onto my face," I pant.

"It's not only the beach that is made of refuse. Our whole island is," brags Huxley. Snot-nosed showoff. "Pala, also known as the Great Pacific Garbage Patch or the Pacific Trash Vortex, is a concentration of marine litter in the central North Pacific Ocean that is twice the size of Texas—and growing daily. The Patch is composed of very high amounts of plastics, chemical sludge, and other debris that have been trapped by the currents of the North Pacific Gyre."

Aloha! Remains of an albatross chick that was accidentally fed plastic by its parents and died. Welcome to paradise.

"I love what you've done with the place!" I bark!

"It's actually what *you've* done with the place," corrects Huxley. "Pala formed as a result of your society's pollution gathered by oceanic currents. It is the first truly modern island: much of it is made of plastic. You see, plastic does not biodegrade like natural debris. Instead it *photodegrades* which means it disintegrates into ever smaller pieces while still remaining plastic. This process continues down to the molecular level. So the plastic ultimately becomes small enough to be ingested by the oceans' many life forms. Thus plastic enters the food chain.

"Larger pieces of plastic end up in the stomachs of animals, and their babies; killing them. Floating plastic can absorb other pollutants dumped into the seawater like DDT and PAHs. The plastics themselves leach toxic chemicals into the water such as bisphenol A, PCBs, and derivatives of polystyrene. Some of these poisons can mimic estrogen, causing hormone disruption in the ingesting animal. Toxic plastic pieces are eaten by jellyfish which are then eaten by larger fish which are then *consumed* by humans resulting in their ingestion of all these harmful chemicals.

"If you can't manufacture a product that doesn't safely and naturally break down, then that product simply ought not to be made."

"Don't be so inflexible, kid. How's about bending over for Daddy?" I bark.

"Only a truly insane society would mass manufacture something that's poisonous and doesn't biodegrade."

"Damaging our planetary life support system on a variety of fronts which has led to the largest wave of species extinctions in sixty-five million years while also endangering humanity itself is a small price to pay for the modern whatever," sayeth Moses.

A horse-drawn wagon clatters its way down a road and stops at the lip of the beach. "You OK there, Hux?" calls the man driving the vehicle.

"Yeah, Papa! I'm fine!" Huxley yells back. "We've got visitors!"

He drops the reins of the workhorses and jumps to the ground. Walking towards us through the trash is a man in his fifties wearing a straw hat, plain shirt, and trousers. "It's the Amish *Sanford and Son*!" I bark!

"Hello. I'm Dev Godknit," greets the man.

"I am The Most Reverend Colonel Bat Guano, U.S. Army Special Third World Serf Incineration Forces, Retired—purebred," I bark!

"I am Moses—specializing in liberation, prophecy, interior design."

"We don't get many strangers around here," says the senior Godknit.

"We're friends of Hellevator. He told us you'd be genial hosts which means all the hookers and blow we want," I bark.

"So get on it, Gomer," addeth Moses.

So we pile in the wagon and head for whoreville. Huxley rides his stallion ahead ostensibly to line up a mountain of blow.

"That's quite the boy you have," I bark to Dev Godknit. "You should bite him on the head. Hard."

"How many children do you have?" asks Moses.

"It depends on what you mean by 'my children.' Biologically speaking, I have only Huxley. Most couples in Pala have between one and three children. Some of course have none. It's quite taboo to have more than three."

"That's 'biologically speaking.' You have other children by a nonbiological route?"

"Indeed. About fifteen of them."

"You've adopted fifteen children?"

"It's not adoption in the way that your modern society institutes adoption programs. Your families, whether biologically produced or socially engineered through adoption organizations, are tightly bottled, suffocating entities. Predestined and compulsory, there is no escape from your modern family. Our society is based on a completely different type of family. Not exclusive, not foreordained, not forced; our families are inclusive and voluntary. Escape is built into our family system.

"We call them Home Mutual Unions."

"*HoMUs* for short!" I bark!

"Each Home Mutual Union consists of ten to twenty assorted couples in the community, their children and extended family. Whenever a home situation becomes distressing, the child is encouraged—by the community—to migrate to one of the other homes in the union. Everybody in the union adopts everybody else.

"If a child feels unhappy in his first home, he has ten to twenty other options—other places and people to give him some space to breathe, some freedom. Meanwhile the father and mother receive some thoughtful guidance from the other members of their union. Generally speaking, after a few weeks of separation to allow for counseling and reflection, the parents and the children are all fit to be with each other again. But it's certainly not only when there are problems in the family that children resort to their deputy parents and grandparents. Children do it all the time whenever they feel the need for a different atmosphere or new experience. But as in any healthy family situation, with rights also come responsibilities. Children, whether staying with parents or deputy parents, are expected to pull their own weight. They have their duties: babysitting the younger children, cleaning up their rooms, picking up dog shit out of the yard (as I ironically and aptly lick my asshole)—our families hinge on responsibilities as well as rights. But not in one of your small, airless, ironically and aptly named *nuclear families*. Responsibilities and rights in a large, open, unpredetermined, mutually embracing family, where many different abilities and talents are represented and cultivated, and children experience all the meaningful things that human beings do and endure—working, playing, loving, getting old, being sick, dying..."

Moses: "My stepfather beat the shit out of me and I turned out just fine."

Guano: "I can vouch for that. Aside from committing

various genocides on the way to the promised land, the guy's a sweetheart. And hung like a sodomy-lovin' mule."

"A Home Mutual Union protects children against abuse and the worst forms of parental incompetence while also increasing responsibility in children by exposing them to a wide variety of child-rearing methods. In your foreordained, closed families, children are sentenced to a long incarceration term under one single set of parental imprisoners. These familial wardens may be honorable and wise, in which case the little prisoners will emerge more or less unscarred. But in reality most of your parental jailers are not markedly good or wise. They're liable to be well-meaning but stupid, or not well-meaning and frivolous, or neurotic, or self-absorbed and selfish, or blatantly malevolent, or just fucking insane. May Providence help the young captives committed by law and custom and religion to their tender mercies! In contrast, here we have large, inclusive, voluntary families. No foreordained jailers. Our children develop in a working microcosm of society at large (unfortunately the same holds true for children in your society): a smaller in scope but accurate realization of the environment in which they're going to have to live when they're grown up."

"Who runs these Home Mutual Unions? Corporations? Government?"

"We don't have corporations. And they aren't run by the government either; government has little place in communal family life. Home Mutual Unions are run by their members. They are cooperatives—just like our larger businesses are. Voluntary associations. Decentralized neighborhood groups that don't inculcate prescribed doctrines: we're not interested in turning out heavily conditioned clones; we're only interested in turning out good human beings. Healthier relationships in more responsible groups, wider sympathies and deeper understandings."

Guano: "That may be so, but you could never force this sort

of thing on the modern world. A minority of decent parents would not allow their children to be co-raised by their maniac neighbors. A majority of maniac parents would frown upon their children being infested with anything but their own perverted beliefs and psychological maladies."

Moses: "What if the maniac parents were just as lazy as your average modern sluggard? I would think pawning the *enfants terribles* off on the neighbors would be terribly *merveilleux*."

Guano: "But they'd never want to take responsibility for *someone else's* little brat. No. If you don't want to have anything to do with your lil' imp (standard parenting procedure) it's far easier to send it to school for most of the day; the rest of the time the television can raise it (standard parenting procedure)."

Moses: "That's unfair. A modern child can be raised by many other forms of mass media besides the TV."

"Home Mutual Unions don't need to be forced on the people of our communities. They are the organic outgrowths of our communities. This is the natural way for our society to exist. We actually depend on our neighbors. We have to. The human population is in balance here with the ecosystem. That means it's not a large population. A lower human population means people are actually valuable, not a hindrance or expendable. It's basic supply and demand. A surplus of humans, as witnessed in the rest of the world, makes humans disposable, as is most everything in your disposable society. But there are no throwaway humans in our society. They are what they should be: valuable resources. Home Mutual Unions are a logical extension of this."

A mile inland from the coast the road ascends steeply up a series of switchbacks. Eventually the horses succeed in pulling us up to the top of a ridge which marks the starkest of lines of demarcation. Behind us, the coastal wasteland of waste. Ahead, a valley teeming with lush tropical vegetation.

I'm held speechless by the bounty of life before me. How

gloriously beautiful the world seems after the darkness of man-made horrors through which I had passed.

Our wagon begins its descent. Waterfalls leaping the whole distance, or broken into smaller cascades. Streams like silver ribbons bordered with green moss. Here and there a deep gorge. Everywhere the wild and luxuriant vegetation of the tropics delights the eye by its beauty and variety. The noble breadfruit tree—its arching branches clothed with its peculiarly rich and glossy foliage, the elegantly shaped casuarina, the lush pandanus, the palms with their stately trunks and green crests of nodding leaves, impart to the scene a character of oriental allure. The sun is shining brilliantly; low down in the east the sky is golden, birds are flying in flocks, screaming and shrieking; while from the trees come melodious pipings and the trills of finches, mingled with deep-toned organ-like notes. An immense valley—mother to it all. Its sides rising grandly and alive, with zigzag paths up the slopes. Far in the distance, amid its shadows, falls the highest and wispiest of cascades. And at its base, a town nestled in a grove of coconuts.

"How is this possible?" Moses asks. "You people live on a floating toxic landfill!"

"Eighty percent of the island is composed of plastic. But some of the remaining refuse decomposes naturally. In fact, some of it makes an acceptable fertilizer. Add a healthy booster of natural topsoil shipped in decades ago by the founding father of Pala, give the ecological system time to balance itself, and you eventually have the reemergence of life."

"Why not ship in some sand to fix up the beaches?"

"Keeping visible garbage on the island boundaries along with a lack of chain eateries is an effective method of modern-overweight-tourist control. We are keen on discouraging the outside world from taking a closer look here. Given what your culture has been about for thousands of years, it's apparent to anyone with eyes that once we're discovered we'll sooner or later be destroyed, with our mutilated remains being assimilated into your Mother Culture."

"But isn't that, and hasn't that always been, *human nature*?"

"Well it certainly has been the way of human history. But God forbid one would have the imagination to envision humanity throwing off the shackles of its own history and changing its course—changing its *culture*, and thereby cultivating and enhancing the parts of human nature that lead to fuller human lives. That's part of what Pala is about: to demonstrate a truly better social structure can make better human beings. Now nobody is naïve enough to believe humanity can ever be perfected. We are mortal, fallible creatures to our core. There may be such a thing as evil in the human makeup. But that doesn't mean humans can't be greatly improved upon from their present predominant form. Human beings *can* be made to live better and more peaceably with themselves and their planet if you give them the social tools to do so and teach them the wisdom of using them."

Our wagon continues down the dirt road, passing alongside terraced hills of rice, corn, and sweet potatoes with a dozen workers tending to them. "This is one of our town's largest farms and businesses," says Godknit. "It's owned and democratically controlled by its workers. That's fundamental in Pala's economic system."

"Which is?"

"Our economy is organized around *real* free market exchange, unlike your modern economic system which is a free market in name only. In reality, the global capitalist market is manipulated through price fixing, collusion, special deals, hidden and not-so-hidden subsidies, tax breaks, etc., etc. In reality, yours is a market dominated and controlled by huge concentrations of capital (corporations) and government which both cooperate and compete with one another.

"Instead of a system controlled by large organizations—private or public—ours is an economy organized around free market exchange between producers, and production is carried out mainly by self-employed artisans and farmers, small producers' cooperatives, worker-controlled large enterprises, and consumers' cooperatives. *Real* free market exchange that is *uncoerced* by the dictates of accumulated capital."

"How do you prevent high concentrations of capital from manipulating the market?"

"By not allowing high concentrations of capital to form in the first place."

"If you have free market exchange, how do you prevent high concentrations of capital from forming?"

"Mainly by one simple rule: the only legitimate standard for establishing property ownership is by way of *use and occupancy.* If a person is not using and occupying a piece of land (including the home and/or business on that land) then the person does not own that land."

Moses: "So if I don't physically work at a business then I can't own a piece of that business? Good God! That means no corporations!"

Guano: "No more buying stock and expecting a piece of what someone else has produced? No more obscene amounts of accumulated capital? Where's the fun in that?"

Moses: "Under the use-and-occupancy rule, what's to stop somebody from claiming your horses and wagon as their own when you stop using them at night?"

"Those things are personal possessions, not property. Personal, movable possessions, like a hammer or a refrigerator, are obviously yours to keep whether you use them or not. *Property* refers to the land, along with the homes and businesses connected to that land. If you use the land you occupy, it's yours. If you live in the house on that land, it's yours. If you work in the business on that land, that business and what it produces are yours. If you don't use and occupy it, it's not yours. If you abandon it, it's no longer yours."

"Can you sell your home here?"

"Of course. It's a free market. You can sell it if you choose. However, the sale of your home does not confer property ownership to the buyer; that buyer must after the sale use and occupy that house for it to be his. If he abandons it or tries to rent it to someone else, he loses the right to call that property his own."

"Can I pay someone to build a house for me on a bit of land I'm going to use and occupy?"

"Again, yes. In a free market, producers and buyers can negotiate any uncoerced deal they choose."

"How do you pay the house builder?"

"Like you would pay for anything else: with money from your savings or with a loan. Different communities have different approaches on issuing no-interest credit to their citizens. One very effective method is the establishment of democratically run not-for-profit banks (like credit unions)—organizations beholden to helping members of their community instead of helping themselves to profits. In fact, our nonprofit community-controlled banks have a much lower bad-debt rate than your conventional capitalist banks because financial co-ops are based on solidarity, and failing to repay a loan from a free-banking initiative is culturally equivalent to stealing from your friends.

"This is no utopia we have here—it's merely a *more just, more equitable* way for humans to live with each other. Misfortunes still happen. Some people still try to take advantage of others. But a community based on economic mutualism works to help its fellow citizens meet their agreed-upon commitments and responsibilities because there's no incentive to want to see them fail. Unlike in capitalism: where the prospect of making a profit by foreclosing on your distressed neighbor brings out the worst in human nature. And you wonder why shortsighted greed is rampant in your society. It's because greed is the bedrock principle on which your economic system is built. The accumulation of more and more *capital* is the very name of your system!

"But here, every person is entitled to the reasonable amount of land they live on, giving them a stake in their own community. Here, the laborer gets the full fruits of his labor. If he works with others, he and his fellow workers democratically decide how to fairly share what's produced. The harder and longer he works, the more he's likely to earn; but thanks to the use-and-occupancy rule, he can't accumulate the capital necessary to divorce any other producer from the means of production."

"So in Pala who owns and controls capital goods (man-made, non-land means of production)?"

"In some places in Pala, capital goods are commonly managed public assets, in other places they are private property. Different communities decide for themselves. Our whole system, including economic system, is largely decentralized. Outside of some basic rules and guidelines, individuals and local communities are empowered to decide what works best for them."

"In your system could I buy a machine used for production and charge others to use it?"

"No. That's an unethical source of income. As Benjamin Tucker saw it: '*the natural wage of labor is its product; this wage, or product, is the only just source of income (leaving out, of course, gift, inheritance, etc.); all who derive income from any other source abstract it directly or indirectly from the natural and just wage of labor...*' This abstracting process generally takes one of two forms—interest and rent; these two constitute usury and are simply different methods of levying tribute for the use of capital; capital simply being stored-up labor which has already received its pay in full, its use ought to be gratuitous; the lender of capital is entitled to its return intact, and nothing more; the only reason why the banker, the stockholder, the landlord, the manufacturer, and the industrialist are able to exact usury from labor lies in the fact that they are backed by legal privilege in your system. But usurers enjoy no legal privilege here in Pala."

Moses: "Benjamin Tucker was also into the nonsensical labor theory of value."

"That was true of Benjamin Tucker. But we're not into blindly following icons here. We follow whatever works best for us. And what makes sense is the subjective theory of value, not the labor theory of value."

"Who invests in an enterprise if they're not entitled to financially profit off it?" asks Moses.

"Individuals invest in their own businesses since they are the ones who benefit by it. Same goes for groups of workers banding together in collective business endeavors. The community itself invests in various local enterprises that benefit the community. Our mutual credit institutions allow for equality of opportunity in accessing resources and allow for greater entrepreneurship as well as competition in business enterprises. Investments of labor, time, money, and other resources are made every day here. But not by parasites expecting to profit from an endeavor they themselves are not going to labor for."

I bark, "Interest is taboo here. So is rent. How can one expect to receive a proper economic anal fisting?"

Moses asks, "But profits themselves are not taboo here, yes?"

"Are you using Adam Smith's technical definition of profit? Smith said: *The profit or gain of capital is altogether different from the wages of labor.* Earnings made by laborers in full control of all they produce who are freely exchanging with other such laborers—all completely uncoerced—are legitimate.

Everything outside of these wages of labor (except gifts, inheritance, etc.) is unethical."

"And this works?"

"It works well if a fair, decent society is your goal. It works well if a sustainable economy at the heart of a sustainable society is your goal. It works well if you want to create people who can both fairly compete and cooperate with each other. It does not work well if your goal is to create an economic system in which two percent of the planet's population owns over half of the entire world's wealth, and fifty percent of the planet's population owns virtually none of the world's wealth—with the gap between haves and have-nots continuing to widen rapidly. It works poorly if you want to create a multitude of greedy, shortsighted drones and clones intent on acquiring as much as they can as quickly as they can at their fellow man's and planet's expense."

Our wagon rolls past another farm where a tractor is plowing the earth. "You use motorized equipment here?" asks Moses.

"Yes. Motorized equipment. Electricity. Running water. Basic home appliances. A good health care system for all. Some of us even use automobiles."

"I thought you fuckers were Amish. The only reason I moved here is to scam you into building me a barn," I bark.

"In Pala we use and develop technology. *But* we have always chosen to adapt our technology to human beings—not our human beings to technology. What we can afford technologically is dictated by our wish to be happy, our ambition to become fully human.

"That may be *the* most fundamental difference between our societies. In Pala, we are always cognizant of the destructive, dehumanizing side of technology. We would rather err on the side of conservatism and not incorporate a technological advancement than plunge heedlessly ahead. This specific cultural divide between Pala and your modern society is truly immense and unbridgeable because your modern society stands diametrically opposed to us—you blindly and recklessly leap ahead in your mad pursuit of ever greater technology. You never pause to think on the paradoxical fact that the advent of many *good* technologies adds up to a very *bad* result. And that perhaps adding more seemingly *good* technologies will only make your situation *worse*. Indeed, when you analyze it, your whole modern world's ideology is continued and constant technological progress, and the further centralization of society that goes with it. Your religious differences, political differences, economic differences—all these and the others are of secondary importance. Because you all share a common goal: technological progress. That is your true ideology.

"But not ours."

"What *is* your ideology?"

"To protect and nurture the balance of life. That means *all* life in our home. Our home being this planet. It is our life support system. And since all planetary life is connected, protecting the balance of life means protecting ourselves. For we humans cannot survive without this interconnected web of life."

"Are you vegetarian pussies here?" I bark.

"Many Palanese are vegans or vegetarians. Some eat meat. We all must kill in order to survive. It's just a question of limits. Unfortunately, limits are not embraced by your modern society."

"I like meat. Hard 'n hot. And hard. That's on my résumé," I bark, showing him my résumé.

Closer now, in the midst of this lovely valley, rich in fruit-bearing trees and cultivated fields, is an almost English-looking village, with its cottages and gardens, its local stores and farmers' markets—all that speak of a simple home life. "Welcome to Mencken," announces Godknit.

Our wagon reaches the valley floor, crossing a small wooden

bridge spanning a stream so clear that every pebble in its gravelly bed is visible. Troops of children are pursuing their sports in every direction. Some wading in the stream, some sailing tiny boats, or actively spattering one another with water, a recreation which they enjoy without fear of damage to clothing, since they wear largely none. "Kiddie-porn dungeon!" I bark! Some children, a few scarcely old enough to walk, swim about in the deeper places, like amphibious creatures. Some swing on ropes of sennit, suspended from the branches of trees, while others quietly sit in the shade making bouquets and wreaths of wildflowers. Among them all is not a single overweight child.

"Where are all your fatties?" I bark!

"We have no obese people in Pala. Unlike your modern society, we do not live sedentary existences or eat heavily processed foods. Food here is grown naturally and locally, comprised mostly of fruits and vegetables. Most everyone grows food gardens of their own. Many help on the larger farms at harvest time. People here are intimately connected with their environment, and that begins with food. Correspondingly, we love being outdoors. We swim, we hike, we climb, we explore. We don't huddle indoors, enslaved by narrow professional specializations during work time, and electronic gadgets or some other mass media wizardry during our leisure time."

"You don't have specialized professional fields here?"

"Yes, we do have them. But, as specialization is a facet of technologization, we have limits. As a society becomes ever more specialized, the more it loses sight of any broader perspective. A professional man—which is what your modern society breeds—tends to see things from the frame of reference of his specialty, which his life revolves around, and loses count of whatever falls outside this narrow field. Yes, a specialized vision allows for a much sharper focus. But the narrower and more specialized a vision, the more the periphery—the larger picture—becomes impossible to see.

"Through this narrowed professional deformation, mad obsession with technology and its trinkets, and his own warped reasoning, your modern man has become blind, fractured, alienated, detached—detached from his surroundings, and in the end, detached from what it is to be human.

"And part of what it is to be human is to be *physical.* A healthy physical body is imperative in creating sane, whole human beings. You don't see morbidly obese animals in nature, and yet your culture churns out these humanlike monstrosities by the hundreds of millions. Hordes and hordes of grotesque feeders. Only a society so unnatural from top to bottom could produce humans so physically unnatural. All of which is neatly matched by your average modern's *mental* state.

"It's all linked. As cliché as it is, it's nevertheless true: Life is a balance. Healthy bodies allow for healthy minds. A specialist balancing their professional pursuit with other intellectual challenges outside of their narrow specialization is customary here and helps nurture broader perspectives. Further, our fields of specialization are not life sentences. Many specialists wind up changing professions, sometimes many times over the course of a life; and our society greatly encourages this. No one should ever be pigeonholed in one occupation. How monotonous and damaging to the human psyche."

"Welcoming people to change their professional fields must slow progress in those fields."

"Indeed it does. And as discussed earlier, we would sooner sacrifice progress in any one field for the progress of the human individual. Happy, healthy individuals make a happy, healthy society; the progress of specialization has nothing to do with it, as demonstrated by your world.

"All this, with a lot of physical play and some good old-fashioned manual labor, keeps even our most intellectual specialists grounded in a grounded society. In Pala even a professor, even a government official, generally puts in an hour of manual labor each day. As part of his pleasure."

"You have a small population. How many professional fields of specialization do you have?"

"Certainly far fewer than your modern society. We've never had the need for the many specializations spawned by your capitalist system that are purely driven by greed and thus are almost universally antihuman. Marketing and advertising come immediately to mind. And we have only very limited interest in the many specializations largely driven by the process of technologization and thus are prone to be more useful in centralizing power than helping humans. For example, we have little practical need for research in physics and chemistry since we have few heavy industries to be made more competitive, none of your armaments to be made more infernal. We concentrate on the research which does us the greatest good—in the science of life and mind. You people are irretrievably committed to applied physics and chemistry, with all their dismal consequences, military, political, and social. The world's underdeveloped countries aren't committed. They don't have to follow your example. They're still free to take the road we've taken—the road of applied biology, the road of fertility control and the limited production and selective industrialization which fertility control makes possible, the roads that lead towards happiness from the inside out, through health, through awareness, through a change in one's attitude towards the world; not towards the mirage of happiness from the outside in, through toys and pills and nonstop distractions. They could still choose our way; but they don't want to, they want to be exactly like you, God help them. They're foredoomed to frustration and disappointment, predestined to the misery of enslavement.

"In this, the Third World and Modern World are united. Despite your specious headlines in your mass media, there are no culture wars being fought. Your Mother Culture has won and has an imperious hold on human civilization.

"That is until the day Pala rises to fight you."

"I thought you people were gluten-free pacifists! With, quote: '*none of your [modern world's] armaments...*'"

"We have none of your modern world's armaments. But we're not pacifists. We avoid violence, because violence is only effective in very limited circumstances and should only be resorted to when there are no other viable options. But given that violence against life is what your culture is based on, and given that you use violence so readily (violence, both physical and psychological, against humanity and the rest of the living world) we would be fools to cede the option of violence to your side only. We would be fools not to defend ourselves. Such are the circumstances we find ourselves in."

"Are you going to send them a poisoned pūpū platter?" I bark!

"You could build them an Amish barn with no doors. That would be mean," suggesteth Moses.

"Not as amusing as building them an Amish barn with toxic drywall from China," suggests Godknit.

"Ha!"

"Ha!"

"Ha!"

"No, really, how you gonna kill all the cretins?" I bark!

"And how can I get in on this?" asks Moses. "I'm always up for a good righteous genocide."

"We aren't going to kill anyone. There are simply too many of them to kill for that strategy to be plausible and effective. Humanity's population is so out of control that you literally have billions upon billions of parasites on the beleaguered planetary system. No. What you need to do is *change* them. And humanely reduce their numbers. But such a discussion is for another time. We're almost home."

Our wagon proceeds up a neighborhood street of neat and

light-built dwellings dotting the side of a mountain slope. The thatching of the cottages, bleached to an almost snowy whiteness, offers a pleasing contrast to the surrounding verdure. We pass various neighbors working their gardens or helping each other with small jobs around the home or reading books or napping under the shade of trees. Many of the women, especially the younger ones, wear simple skirts with light blouses that leave their midriffs bare. The men are generally in lightweight shorts or trousers with liberally unbuttoned shirts or no shirts at all. The neighbors wave to Godknit, some looking inquisitively at Moses, others looking more askew. "Don't worry," Godknit assures Moses. "They're all well-meaning. We just don't get visitors here."

"I look forward to your public stoning," I assure Moses.

We reach a fine avenue of well-grown trees running along the crest of a hill leading to a cottage prettily situated upon a green knoll and overshadowed by wide-branching breadfruit trees. "Here we are," announces Godknit.

"Bring on the hookers!" I bark!

A tall, slender woman waves from the front door.

"That's what I'm talking about!" I bark, humping Moses' leg as he hops out of the wagon.

"Mom got home early from work!" says Huxley, bounding from the house towards us.

"Your mother's work is hooking? This is paradise!" I bark!

"I told Mom about our guests. She's got dinner already made," says Huxley to his father, who hands the boy the reins of the horses.

"Thanks, Hux. Go feed and water the horses. Then wash up. We'll hold up on dinner for you," says senior Godknit.

"Take your time, kid. I won't be able to eat till I've climbed that mountain of blow anyway. And perhaps your mother," I bark!

The elegant middle-aged woman greets us at the door.

"Welcome to Pala, and our home. I'm Ashlee Hinderloss."

"And this is God's law bringer, called Moses. I'm his pussy magnet, called pussy magnet—purebred," I bark, completing the introductions.

The interior of the cottage matches the exterior in neatness and agreeable simplicity. A hybridization: farmhouse vernacular architecture with Polynesian building materials. The furniture is suitable for comfortable living—several carved wooden chairs, a matching dining table, the family couch, bookshelves filled with books that look as if they've actually been read. Basic appliances are found throughout the house—a small electric stove and refrigerator in the kitchen along with a sink for washing dishes, toilet and shower in the bathroom, a ceiling fan in each of two bedrooms, lamps where warranted. "No television!" I bark!

"Television is one modern 'wonder' we Palanese can't afford," says Ashlee.

"Or just don't want," adds Dev.

"No computers either?" asks Moses.

"There are computers used in schools, especially in university work that deals in research. Our government uses them too. You'll find them in businesses as well. But most Palanese are too busy living their everyday concrete realities to lose themselves in a virtual reality at home with a home computer," she explains.

"No television, not much home-computer use—how do you inform the populace without mass media?" Moses asks.

"And how do you brainwash the populace without mass media?" I bark.

"We do have various methods of disseminating information," Dev says. "Most Palanese communities have several newspapers. Not anything like *your* major newspapers, of course, with their built-in bias for the modern system, one-sidedness, lack of any deep and real reasoning. Even in your supposedly *best* big-circulation newspapers, issues such as global warming, government versus corporations, and terrorism are portrayed as root issues and not symptoms of a highly centralized, highly technologized mass culture so perverse that it's bent on enslaving itself via its technology in a best-case scenario, destroying itself via its technology in the worst case. The invested interests directing your society offer their 'answers' for curing these never-ending symptoms, 'answers' which your newspapers and other mass media outlets faithfully present to the public. 'Answers' that are always the same: more government intervention is needed to better control all these evil corporations and terrorists! or maybe the government is the problem and should be emasculated! (with the power vacuum being presumably filled by even more big-business influence). Or that ever-popular answer disputed by no sensible modern: even better and greater technology is the answer to the problem! All the while any real examination of the actual root problems and the subsequent authentic solutions which can only be had after careful and concentrated analysis are simply not presented to the public. In this way, your mass news media set the agenda for the modern status quo, and the invested interests directing your society continue to be able to manufacture consent from a brainwashed populace."

"But you digress, honey," smiles Ashlee at her husband. "Unlike the modern world's corporate newspapers, Palanese newspapers have a panel of editors representing several different perspectives and interests. Each of them gets space for comment and criticism. This leaves the reader in a better position to form a more complete understanding of what's at play, and ultimately to make up their own mind on what the best solution is."

Dev: "Even more important: Unlike your major newspapers, our newspapers usually read like a philosophical discourse. Because, after all, society's real root issues are philosophical.

And any decent solutions can only be found by using logic to its reasonable end to construct policies that resonate with your society's values. Along those lines, if you have a society with a wise value system, wise answers to societal dilemmas can usually be found."

Moses: "There is no way a modern big-circulation newspaper could get away with philosophical discussions posing as news."

Dev: "But that really *is* the news! Anything besides the root problems and your philosophy on how to deal with them is mere triviality. Our citizenry expects its news like this because they're taught to critically analyze everything, to use logic as best as possible to a reasonable end—our citizenry is taught how to *critically think*. It's at the heart of Pala's school system—teaching methods of critical thought, from kindergarten through the highest levels of university. If you're interested, I can show you one of our schools tomorrow."

"Oh, so you're the schoolyard pedophile?" I bark.

"Worse. I'm a teacher," Dev laughs.

"To get back to our conversation on ways Pala informs itself of news," says Ashlee, "as important as newspapers is our town hall meeting. Not the ugly, farcical town hall shouting matches pitting ignoramus against ignoramus that have become popular in your world. Pala's communities are much smaller—and much better educated in the underlying contexts that frame and give meaning to events—allowing us to use town hall meetings to not only discuss our issues, but also decide on action through the voting process. Pala is largely a direct democracy."

Dev says: "Our political system is naturally akin to our economic system. Our largest businesses are worker-controlled cooperatives. Every employee gets an equal say in the decisions of the company through voting. Now that's not to say every worker gets *paid* the same amount. Obviously, as in life, some people are more talented than others. Some have acquired special skills through years of education and training. Ashlee is a surgeon at our community's hospital. She gets paid more than the janitor at the hospital. As she should. She's put in more time training than the janitor, and her skills are in shorter supply than that of a janitor. *But* how much Ashlee gets paid and how much the janitor gets paid is decided equally by Ashlee, the janitor, and the rest of the workers at the hospital. Some people may be more valuable because of their unique skills and intelligence, but all people in our society have an equal say in the course our society takes."

"Oh! Just like in a modern democracy!" I bark!

"Ha!"

"Ha!"

"Ha!"

"Ha!"

Ashlee: "The workers decide how their business is run, how to distribute what is produced, and how to divide what is earned. But the enterprise is still a completely voluntary association. If I'm not happy with the decisions my fellow coworkers make, I'm free to seek an opportunity at another hospital cooperative or set up business for myself. This holds true in Pala's political system as well. Individuals decide for themselves just how much or how little they'll participate. But each person has an equal say on all issues affecting them and their community. If an individual or group isn't happy with the decisions democratically made by the community, they're free to leave to form their own community with its own standards."

Dev: "This idea of voluntary association permeates many facets of our public life. For example, many of our community services are paid for by user fees and not government. Public services like electricity and water are naturally based on user fees. If an individual wants the use of those services, he pays the fee. If he does not want the service, he doesn't pay. Our roads are built along these lines using toll money. Those wishing to use the road pay the fee. Those who do not wish to use it are not compelled to pay anything."

Moses: "Voluntary association is all well and good, but do you expect me to believe you've engineered a way around the need for government here in Pala?"

"No," answers Dev. "Anarchism is a lovely ideal, and it should always be the goal for any society. But it's naïve to believe that ideal can ever be fully reached. As long as there is a finite amount of resources and human nature is what it is, there will be a need for government. Something stronger than voluntary associations is required in key areas of community life. We have government to provide free schooling, including postgraduate studies. We have government to provide universal health care—and free birth control to all Palanese. Such things as a police force, firefighters, and a court system are necessary and should never be privatized."

"Our police force and court system are very small and seldom needed. Most disputes can be successfully mediated in our Home Mutual Unions," adds Ashlee.

"And our government is much smaller and far less intrusive than those found in your modern society," says Dev. "Government, and institutions in general, can be kept small and innocuous when you have a small population in balance with the surrounding ecology and when you have a society in control of its technology and industries instead of the other way around."

"Which means you have less technology," says Moses.

"So be it. That's a tradeoff we've *gladly* made," says Dev. "The more complex a society, the more government is necessary to coordinate it. So we have limited industries with a decentralized political and economic system which means we have little need for a government to coordinate and control an intricate setup of industry, economy, and bloated human population. A smaller, simpler society comprised of highly educated people means a sustainable society with much more freedom."

"The major purpose of the American government is to coordinate and feed the massive military-industrial complex," Ashlee affirms.

A dog called Guano: "The military-industrial complex is nothing more than the gigantor state-subsidized R & D infrastructure created for private corporate economic interests. The legalized grift worth hundreds of billions of dollars per year works as such: public funds are siphoned into the private research and development of new technologies that sometimes make fine weapon systems and always make private corporations shitloads of money after these private corporations receive government funding to develop the new technologies and then take the new technologies developed at the cost of the taxpaying public and sell it back to the public in some new gizmo at a tidy profit since any costs of developing the technologies were already previously paid for by the public."

"We obviously have nothing like a military-industrial complex in Pala," says Ashlee. "Our government does not use public funds to privately research and develop evil technologies used to kill and control, technologies later sold back to a public which already paid for them. With no government-sponsored war and technology machinations to pay for, our government remains small and our taxes are very low compared to what you endure in your modern society."

Dev: "A smaller, simpler society means the individual retains more power. A smaller, simpler society of highly educated people means real democracy."

Ashlee: "Our citizens use town hall meetings to inform themselves, discuss the issues, and eventually vote on action. This manner of governing is impossible in your world because an incredibly complex society of billions of people *must* have large organizations to manage the thing. There are millions of decisions to be made every day. The individual cannot possibly make them. So the individual loses control over the many decisions that will affect his life. This leads to great psychological insecurity; a pervasive feeling of impotence and frustration. Such is the terrible compromise you've made for unrestrained technologization and breeding."

"This floating garbage dump is twice the size of Texas," I bark complimentarily. "Are there towns and individuals spread throughout the entire area?"

"Yes. We have a wide range of small communities dotting the land."

"And there's nothing beyond the local politics of your direct democracy? What happens if a community on the north side of the island does something that affects all the communities on the south side?" I bark.

"Pala is a big place, but our communities still communicate with one another and work together," Dev says.

"Pala is so large geographically that it has three major bioregions," Ashlee says.

"Bioregionalism is a political, cultural, and environmental system or set of views based on naturally defined areas called bioregions, or ecoregions," Wikipedia says. "Bioregions are defined through physical and environmental features, including watershed boundaries and soil and terrain characteristics. Bioregionalism stresses that the determination of a bioregion is also a cultural phenomenon, and emphasizes local populations, knowledge, and solutions."

"Pala has three major bioregions," Ashlee says. "When the need arises, our local communities can call for a bioregional convention. Temporary representatives are elected by the local communities to meet with each other to discuss issues that affect the three bioregions comprising the island's ecosystem. Instead of arbitrary state lines based on myths and brute force, political bioregions are the natural, logical way to form political unions on the larger regional level."

Dev says: "But these bioregional conventions are only occasionally called, mostly just to keep our lines of communication open and relationships strong. There just aren't that many regional issues to remedy. Due to our low population and modest industries, resources are easily managed on the local level with few conflicts or crises developing. Further, our economic system with its use-and-occupancy rule limits human greed because one can acquire only the amount of resources that one can use, and no more. With the amount of land and resources an individual can acquire limited, there's no economic incentive to amass disproportionate wealth. Cooperation and limited competition are built into the system; greed is not."

Ashlee says: "So our businesses have no incentive to degrade the environment for the sake of a buck. Also, our economic system compels all business enterprises to be locally owned and operated. You're far less likely to use toxins in your business if you're the one who's got to live next door to that business."

Huxley enters through the front door. "Horses are fed."

"Thanks, Hux," says Dev. "Wash up. Dinner's ready."

The meal is comprised of chicken and soy in a curry sauce with a variety of vegetables, fruit on the side with chocolate, all locally grown and produced. I make polite dinner conversation by barking: "How do you take your fucking here in Pala?"

"Hopefully like we take the other parts of life—healthfully and well!" laughs Ashlee.

"We are very open and honest about sex in Pala," informs Dev. "And why shouldn't we be? Sex is wonderful; an important part of life; a basic need that helps to make life worth living."

Ashlee continues: "In Pala, we discuss sex with our children at an early age. If you give children valid information and treat them with respect, they'll generally grow into adults who make good life decisions. On the other hand if you hide the ways of life from them, mystify things, make life taboo and dirty, you'll have children who never grow up and make decisions you'd expect from children who've never grown up."

"Please demonstrate by fellating the hot oblong vegetables on Daddy's plate," I command Ashlee.

"We teach our children that sex can sometimes be just a fun fling done on a whim, but it can also be a vital tool in building deep feelings of love and affection between people, all depending on the circumstances and individuals involved," Ashlee says.

"Yeah. Sometimes sex can bring two in-tune lovers to a profound understanding of themselves and each other. A meaningful, beautiful moment of lucidity and openness to their existence. Or so I'm told," young Huxley informs with a smirk. "And sometimes people just like to pork each other."

"Well done, my lad," I bark, sizing up whether his leg is of age yet.

Dev: "Like everything else in Pala, we strive to make sex something that's liberating, the reverse of what it is in your modern society."

"You are misinformed on this front. Everybody is free to fuck everybody and everything in modern society. And pork away they do!" I bark!

"Indeed," agrees Dev. "Which is part of the method of control. Modern society is very sexually promiscuous. You constantly fuck each other indiscriminately. Your mass media are saturated with cheap, tawdry images of sex. And like anything else (technology certainly included), being inundated with something that starts out seemingly good inevitably turns into an imprisoning situation. The more extreme your promiscuity becomes, the less it's possible for your citizenry to develop and maintain deeper, more meaningful relationships. In your modern world of instant gratification, sex has become just that—another superficiality to pacify and tranquilize, another distraction. And all the while the other things needed for a serious, giving relationship—such as commitment—fall by the wayside.

"All this is very good for any State that seeks easy control of the people. Childlike citizens addicted to facile pleasures are eminently rulable—as long as they get their continual fix of titillations, they'll want nothing more than to remain inebriated slaves. Conversely, couples who fall deeply in love do unruly things, like swearing their allegiance to each other over that of a flag."

"Yours is a *Brave New World*," Huxley says to me.

"In so many facets, that book was absolutely prescient on what modern society has become and where it is most certainly headed," nods Dev.

"You are amusing yourselves to death," adds Ashlee.

"But while unthinking promiscuity is permitted with a wink, your conventional mores and laws still validate only one type of union: the monogamistic marriage. As if that institution hasn't always been a recipe for sexual repression and dysfunction!" Dev laughs.

"Does that mean you are sweet 'n nutty polygamists?" I bark.

Dev: "Palanese are *individuals*. Our society is geared to helping its people decide for themselves what works best in all matters in life, including sex. As emotionally mature adults, some couples choose monogamy. Other couples feel it's natural to have multiple lovers."

Ashlee: "The Palanese value system is radically different from that of the modern world. And this naturally pertains to sex. From birth on, our people are raised in an environment where sex is viewed very differently than how it's viewed in your culture. There is no stigma attached to sex here. It's just a natural function of life, through and through."

Dev: "Even in many of modern society's so-called open marriages where other lovers are invited into the bedroom, there are problems of jealousy because those couples have been raised from the start in your culture of sexual possessiveness. But nobody possesses anybody else in Pala and this certainly applies to sex. Here, when a partner in a union takes a lover outside the union it's done in the open; there's no sneaking around and deceit, which will kill any relationship; it's not a slight against anyone. It's just acknowledging that humans are attracted to various other humans. Instead of repressing these feelings, which has made miserable human beings for millennia, many Palanese just enjoy flings."

"Is sex with your loving long-term partner better? I think so," says Ashlee. "But for some, sex just for fun with other lovers can have its place too."

Dev: "The important thing in any relationship, one that involves sex or not, is that the people involved are growing together. If one person is going one way and the other person is going another, the relationship will soon have no common footing. That's part of the reason marriages fail on the massive scale they do in your culture. The husband and wife become detached from each other, if they were ever really attached in the first place. When there's no commonality, there is no basis for relationship.

"And it's not hard to see why so few of your people grow together. It's your ideology of rapid technologization coupled with the global capitalist economic engine driving the process: a combination that puts technological progress and wealth accumulation ahead of humans; a combination that, more than ever, uproots families, detaching its members from each other.

"Technology and global capitalism are creating a world that changes exponentially rapidly. You can't make rapid, drastic changes in the technology and the economy of a society without causing rapid changes in all other aspects of the society as well, and such rapid changes inevitably break down traditional values.

"The breakdown of traditional values to some extent implies the breakdown of the bonds that hold together traditional small-scale social groups, marriages and families included. The disintegration of small-scale social groups is also promoted by the fact that modern conditions often require or tempt individuals to move to new locations, separating themselves from their communities. Beyond that, your modern technological society *has to* weaken family ties and local communities if it is to function efficiently. In modern society an individual's loyalty must be first to the system and only secondarily to a small-scale community (despite laughable politically correct lip service to the contrary), because if the internal loyalties of small-scale communities were stronger than loyalty to the system, such communities would pursue their own advantage at the expense of the system."

Ashlee: "What the excitable love of my life was getting at before his slightly tangential Unabomber explosion (ha!) is that, by its nature, your highly technologized society with its global economy uproots families and breaks down marriages. Economic demands often force your people to move around a lot. People who are separated from each other almost certainly cannot grow together in any deep, genuine way. Correspondingly, nowadays both husband and wife are usually compelled to work. Their jobs often require them to spend long hours away from each other. They run in their different circles with different colleagues and different friends. Fertile grounds for couples to grow apart."

Dev: "Plus, with your culture being based on instant pleasures and ever more sensational diversions, it's no wonder modern man is ever more flighty and superficial—not the stuff that individuals capable of healthy long-term relationships are made of."

"Back to the narrower topic of sex," says Moses, "I find it hard to believe that sexual jealousy isn't present here. Sexual jealousy is part of human nature."

"Not in our experience. Some, maybe most, of human nature is what the individual and society make of it," answers Dev. "Maybe you only believe sexual jealousy is part of human nature because that's what your Mother Culture has taught you for centuries. But that type of envy has cultural origins, not biological ones. If you raise children to have honest, open, logical viewpoints about sex, and thereby enable them to grow up into empathetic, secure adults who seek relationships with other such adults, then there is little envy. Sexual jealousy to us is akin to being jealous if your friend has other friends. Emotionally secure, fully developed adults just don't think that way."

Ashlee: "One more vital thing regarding sex and mature adults: every person in Pala realizes the critical importance of birth control. It is never overlooked. It's a cornerstone of our culture, universally taught in homes and schools alike. We view contraceptives like we do education—both are tax-supported, provided to all Palanese free of charge by the government. If one is mature enough for sex, then one must be mature enough to use birth control."

Dev: "The planet's ruinous human overpopulation problem stems from modern technology. Modern agriculture technology has made it possible for the Earth to sustain a far denser population than it ever did before. Modern medical technology has made it possible for humans to defeat many of nature's built-in mechanisms that keep population in balance, such as disease."

Ashlee: "Most Palanese believe modern medical care and the ability to grow plenty of food for everyone in society are good uses of technology; but by controlling nature in these areas we Palanese also realize that we *must* control our population to keep it in balance with our environment."

"Life is about making compromises. Wisdom is knowing

what compromises to make and where to draw the line. Your modern society has few limits on use of medical and agricultural technology, and breeding. So your population numbers balloon, prompting you to develop more and more land, destroying the natural habitats of countless other life forms to make room for human farmland, human living spaces, etc.: a vicious cycle that has thrown the entire ecosystem out of balance and promises its eventual collapse, thereby endangering your own survival." Dev finishes with a laugh: "This *is not* wisdom."

Ashlee: "But we Palanese *have* compromised. We use technology to cure disease, we use technology to farm the land to produce a surplus of food, but we limit our population and thereby limit the amount of land we use for farmland and human development to allow the other animals and plants of our environment to live. It's a compromise that has led to a sustainable society, and truthfully, a healthier, happier society as well."

Dev: "At this point in history, humanity has only two sustainable choices. One: use technology to manipulate nature to grow more food and live longer lives, *and* use technology to *effectively* reduce and control its fertility. Or two: don't use technology in any of those areas and let nature take care of it."

Moses: "The modern world believes there is still the third choice of using technology to grow more food and extend lives but not implementing it to effectively inhibit unrestrained fertility."

Dev: "That *is* a third choice. But it's certainly not a *sustainable* choice."

Ashlee: "Whether, where, when, and how to use technology is obviously a serious, central question. In fact, it is *the* question of our times. A question that can only be successfully addressed by farsighted, ably equipped adults."

"Electricity minus heavy industry plus birth control equals

democracy and plenty. Electricity plus heavy industry minus birth control equals misery, totalitarianism, and war," chips in Huxley.

"Exactly!" blurts Moses. "How do you get a people who can ably make such thought-involving decisions? How do you get a people *worthy* of democracy?"

Ashlee: "It has to happen on a variety of fronts. Wise parenting, community involvement in helping to raise the children, an economic system that gives equal opportunities to everyone, an economic system that ensures everyone has a fair stake in their own community—all active ingredients that help form secure, self-actualized individuals. Also critical: an education system that teaches children how to critically think."

Dev: "Teaching people how to critically think is vital—secure individuals who are given the tools to use logic well will usually come up with good decisions on their own, and when they face problems, usually solve them on their own."

Ashlee: "Humans *can* be more responsible if you raise them in stable, loving situations; if they grow to be confident individuals because they understand their society really does value them as opposed to just paying them lip service to keep them in line and exploited; if you teach them how to use their minds, to use logic to a reasonable end."

Dev: "Population control and equitable access to property and resources through use and occupancy create a society that genuinely values its people—a society that values people over technology, not the other way around, and therefore better controls technology, not the other way around. These are the cornerstones of a *good* society. And education is the cement holding it together: what you teach your population, the techniques you give them to hone their powers of perception and decision-making skills, the values you instill.

"*A population in balance, a fair and sustainable economy, and proper schooling.* That schooling you'll see tomorrow."

"There's something from last night's discussion that bothers me," Moses says, squinting at Dev in the bright morning sunlight as we walk Huxley to school. "Maybe you do have better humans here, but even couples composed of reasonable, intelligent people can grow apart. Relationships *will* die. One of the reasons for government sanctioning marriage is to set rules for when marriages disintegrate."

Dev replies: "First of all, the state has no place in codifying what is and what is not a viable union. A couple should decide that for themselves. Secondly, we don't need large organizations like your state or institutional religions to sanctify our unions. Like everything else here, our unions are completely voluntary. And personal. It's a union of two individuals. If one individual is unhappy and really wants out, that union is void."

"Which brings me back to my point: Government sanctions marriage so that when that modern marriage goes down the shitter, as they inevitably do nowadays, splitting up the finances and kids is easier. It disrupts society less because there's a standardized legalized procedure for these legalized standardized unions," Moses says. "So here in Pala, only the two individuals in the union validate their union—society is kept out of it. But what happens when they split up? Who gets the cash and who's left with the screaming brats?"

"The couple works it out for themselves."

"Can they? Most modern couples end up viciously hating each other. They can't even equitably work together *before* a nasty breakup, let alone during one."

"That's because your society breeds *children*. Ours breeds

adults. In Pala, only rarely can a splitting couple not agree on how to part amicably, or at least fairly. When they can't manage for themselves, we have a court system, but it's not often needed. The couple and the couple's Home Mutual Union can usually work things out.

"The only way our type of society is able to work is because we've raised a society of grown-ups. We raise adults so we can live in more freedom. A society not ruled by large institutions gives the individual much more freedom, but will succeed only if the individual and individuals collectively are up to the *responsibility* of freedom. If we whine and take advantage of each other like spoiled brats, our society will collapse because we have no large authoritarian social structures to keep brats in line.

"*You* authentically need large authoritarian social structures to keep the brats in line. Your modern society creates emotional cripples, psychologically stunted children in adult bodies. Could it be any other way, given your culture's real values? The values we hold and impress upon our young are very different than yours, as you'll continue to see in school."

Dev kisses Huxley on the cheek at the classroom door. "Have a good day, Hux."

"You too, Papa."

The middle-aged man smiles at his son, then walks us further down the school's hallway. "The classroom where I teach is a few doors down."

"You don't teach Huxley's class?" asks Moses.

"No. I teach older students. Although obviously I teach Huxley when he gets home. And not just because I'm a professional teacher. All parents in Pala realize that education isn't just the school's job. In fact, most teaching should come from the home and Home Mutual Union. And this doesn't just pertain to children. Full-grown adults should always be learning as well. Education is a lifelong process with no finish line.

You're either evolving or you're stagnating. But I suppose that's one of the many reasons so few in your culture see it as their job to be teachers to their children. The parents have stagnated for so long they really have nothing to teach."

"Not true! There's never a shortage of myths to teach based on lies, oppression, and stupidity," I bark as American flags fly from millions of assholes.

"It is the individual's task to differentiate himself from all the others and stand on his own feet. All collective identities...interfere with the fulfillment of this task. Such collective identities are crutches for the lame, shields for the timid, beds for the lazy, nurseries for the irresponsible..." says Carl Jung as national flags, religious symbols, etc. fly from billions of assholes.

Dev: "Our culture deems it imperative that everyone has time to themselves in order to read challenging works, observe the world around them, and reflect. This is the lifelong education for self-actualized individuals. Palanese are continually encouraged to critically analyze their world, their own beliefs, their own lives—and when necessary, to *change* their opinions and the ways they live according to the circumstances. This is how people continue to evolve and grow."

"You're saying modern culture is afraid to throw off the dead hand of the past?"

"Your modern culture throws off the dead hand of the past only if it's concerning the progress of technology or business. In all other areas, cowardice and laziness rule. You show me one modern individual skilled and brave enough to continually challenge everything in his world—including his own beliefs and to change those beliefs when they no longer make sense—and I'll show you ten million other moderns who haven't changed since their childhood. Craven indolent clones content to stagnate."

We stop at the door at the end of the hall. "Your classroom?"

asks Moses.

"No. It's the principal's office."

"You cannot prove I blew up the boys' room toilet and boys," I bark.

In the office a slender woman in her forties greets us. "So these are our guests? I'm the school principal, Chandra Narayan. Pleased to meet you," she says, smiling and shaking the hand of Moses. I decide whether to fight or flight or ejaculate. She continues the introductions: "And this is Mr. Crome Scogan, advisor and friend to Pala's secretary of education." Scogan, who resembles an extinct bird-lizard of the Tertiary, pats me on the head. Good enough. Ejaculate it is!

"You are now finally in some capable hands," Dev says to us with a wink. "Time for me to go teach a class. It was a pleasure meeting you. I wish you the best of luck."

"You're the one who needs luck with Huxley running around. You're aware he'll eat you in your sleep?" I bark.

Narayan and Scogan escort us down the hall to a classroom of young children. "Please pardon the interruption, Mrs. Anand," says the principal to the white-haired teacher at the head of the class.

"No trouble at all," answers Mrs. Anand as her boys and girls continue to scribble in their notebooks.

With the teacher resuming her lecture in the background, Moses asks, "What are they studying?"

"Elementary ecology," the principal whispers. "We always begin with ecology. Never give children a chance of imagining that anything exists in isolation. Make it plain from the very start that all living is relationship. Show them relationships in the woods, in the fields, in the ponds and streams, in the village and the country around it. Rub it in.

"We always teach the science of relationship in conjunction with the ethics of relationship. Balance, give and take, no excesses—it's the rule in nature and, translated out of fact into morality, it ought to be the rule among people. Children find it very easy to understand when it's presented to them in a parable about animals. We give them an up-to-date version of Aesop's Fables. Not the old anthropomorphic fictions, but true ecological fables with built-in cosmic morals. We show them photographs of what has happened in China and India, Greece, Africa, America—all the places where stupid, greedy people have tried to take without giving, to exploit without love or understanding. Treat Nature well and Nature will treat you well. Hurt or destroy Nature and Nature will soon destroy you. In a dust bowl, 'Do as you would be done by' is self-evident—much easier for a child to recognize and understand than in an eroded family or village. Psychological wounds don't show—and children know so little about their elders. And, having no standard of comparison, they tend to take even the worst situation for granted, as though it were part of the nature of things. Whereas the difference between ten acres of meadow and ten acres of mountaintop-removal operation is obvious. Environmental degradation is a parable. Confronted by it, it's easy for a child to see the need for conservation and then go on from conservation to morality—easy for him to go on from the Golden Rule in relation to plants and animals and the earth that supports them to the Golden Rule in relation to human beings. The morality to which a child goes on from the facts of ecology and the parables of environmental devastation is a universal ethic. There are no Chosen People in nature, no Holy Lands, no Unique Historical Revelations. Conservation morality gives nobody an excuse for feeling superior or claiming special privileges. 'Do as you would be done by' applies to our dealings with all kinds of life in every part of the world. We shall be permitted to live on this planet only for as long as we treat all nature with compassion and intelligence.

"Ecology leads to empathy. And empathy is *the* basic necessity if the child is to grow into a full-fledged adult—a whole, integrated human being.

"Another essential principle ecology teaches is the law of limited competition."

"Come again?" I bark and do.

"Daniel Quinn defines the law of limited competition as such: You may compete to the full extent of your capabilities, but you may not hunt down your competitors or destroy their food or deny them access to food. In other words, you may compete but you may not wage war on your competitors.

"According to Quinn, humans came into existence following the law of limited competition. This is another way of saying that they lived like all other creatures in the biological community, competing to the full extent of their capacity but not waging war on their competitors. They came into existence following the law and continued to follow the law until about ten thousand years ago when the people of a single culture in the Near East began to practice a form of agriculture in which you were encouraged to wage war on your competitors—to hunt them down, to destroy their food, and to deny them access to food. This was the form of agriculture practiced in your culture, East and West—and is still the form of agriculture practiced in your modern culture today.

"We obviously do not practice this form of agriculture here in Pala for reasons even young children can see."

Mrs. Anand says to her children: "Essentially what the law of limited competition means is that you cannot claim ownership of a disproportionate amount of the food and land. You can fight for food and land, but you cannot act in a genocidal fashion, setting out to kill those who compete with you merely because they compete with you.

"Now, if a species destroys their competitors (Mrs. Anand holds up a photograph of humans in helicopters shooting wolves) then there is more food available to them (she holds up a photo of large-scale farming operations). With more food they can support a higher population (photo of rows of infants). And with a higher population they need more living space, so they expand their territory (photo of bulldozers and modern tract homes). But as they expand their territory they meet more competitors who are eating food that could be theirs (wolves killing a sheep). So they destroy them (wolves being hunted, poisoned, etc.), taking all the food in the new territory for themselves (more farms). With all this new food, their population expands again (more babies) and so does their territory (more tract homes, maybe a swanky strip mall or two or thousand).

"And then it happens all over again. Many different times against many different competitors. This is the way of life for the lawbreakers—those who disregard the law of limited competition. And this way of life works for a short period of time. It doesn't eliminate the lawbreakers instantly. Elimination only takes place when the landscape becomes so dominated by the lawbreakers and the lawbreakers' food that the imbalance topples the entire system." She reiterates: "When the lawbreakers have expanded so far, and have eliminated so many other species, the lack of biodiversity collapses the entire ecosystem. The food chain can withstand only so many holes due to disappearing species. Once enough species are driven to extinction, these holes in the food chain break it. Without balanced biodiversity, there is no working food chain. And with no food chain, the lawbreaker is finally eliminated himself."

Narayan says: "The children grasp the dilemma. A society with ample food can expand its population. If it continues to expand its population, it will need more land to grow more food and exist. If it continues to deprive its competitors of land to grow its population, it will drive its competitors to extinction, breaking the law of limited competition and ensuring its own eventual extinction. The only way to adhere to the law and thus keep your own species alive in the long term is to either limit the amount of food you produce and thereby using Nature to limit your fertility rate, or grow a surplus of food but limit your fertility rate yourselves using birth control methods.

"The indispensability of birth control is taught in school in conjunction with the home and Home Mutual Union. Everyone in Pala understands a healthy, sustainable society must keep its population in balance with the natural environment.

"But ecology and all the vital lessons it imparts is only one of the two pillars on which our entire education system is built. The other pillar is critical thinking." Mrs. Narayan leads us out of the classroom, then continues speaking in the hallway. "Ecology and critical thinking. Naturally the two go hand in hand. Respecting and protecting the interconnected planetary system of life that supports *your* life is simply logical. And logic is a part of critical thinking."

> Wikipedia:
> Critical thinking, in its broadest sense has been described as 'purposeful reflective judgment concerning what to believe or what to do.' The list of core critical thinking skills includes interpretation, analysis, inference, evaluation, explanation, and metacognition. There is a reasonable level of consensus among experts that an individual or group engaged in strong critical thinking gives due consideration to the evidence, the context of judgment, the relevant criteria for making the judgment well, the applicable methods or techniques for forming the judgment, and the applicable theoretical constructs for understanding the problem and the question at hand. In addition to possessing strong critical thinking skills, one must be disposed to engage problems and decisions using those skills. Critical thinking employs not only logic but broad intellectual criteria such as clarity, credibility, accuracy, precision, relevance, depth, breadth, significance, and fairness. The positive habits of mind which characterize a person strongly disposed toward critical thinking include a courageous desire to follow reason and evidence wherever they may lead, open-mind-

edness, foresight attention to the possible consequences of choices, a systematic approach to problem solving, inquisitiveness, fair-mindedness and maturity of judgment, and confidence in reasoning. In reflective problem solving and thoughtful decision making using critical thinking, one considers evidence (like investigating evidence), the context of judgment, the relevant criteria for making the judgment well, the applicable methods or techniques for forming the judgment, and the applicable theoretical constructs for understanding the problem and the question at hand.

'Critical' as used in the expression 'critical thinking' connotes the importance or centrality of the thinking to an issue, question or problem of concern. 'Critical' in this context does not mean 'disapproved' or 'negative.' There are many positive and useful uses of critical thinking, for example formulating a workable solution to a complex personal problem, deliberating as a group about what course of action to take, or analyzing the assumptions and the quality of the methods used in scientifically arriving at a reasonable level of confidence about a given hypothesis. Using strong critical thinking we might evaluate an argument, for example, as worthy of acceptance because it is valid and based on true premises. Upon reflection, a speaker may be evaluated as a credible source of knowledge on a given topic.

Contemporary cognitive psychology regards human reasoning as a complex process which is both reactive and reflective. The deliberation characteristic of strong critical thinking associates critical thinking with the reflective aspect of human reasoning. Those who would seek to improve our individual and collective capacity to engage problems using strong critical thinking skills are, therefore, recommending that we bring greater reflection and deliberation to decision making. John Dewey is just one of many educational leaders who recognized that a curriculum aimed at building thinking skills would be a benefit not only to the individual learner, but to the community and to the entire democracy. In a seminal study on critical thinking and education in 1941, Edward Glaser writes that the ability to think critically involves three things: (1) An attitude of being disposed (state of mind regarding something) to consider in a thoughtful way the problems and subjects that come within the range of one's experiences; (2) Knowledge of the methods of logical inquiry and reasoning; and (3) Some skill in applying those methods. Educational programs aimed at developing critical thinking in children and adult learners, individually or in group problem solving and decision making contexts, continue to address these same three central elements.

Critical thinking calls for a persistent effort to examine any belief or supposed form of knowledge in the light of the evidence that supports it and the further conclusions to which it tends. It also generally requires ability to recognize problems, to find workable means for meeting those problems, to gather and marshal pertinent (relevant) information, to recognize unstated assumptions and values, to comprehend and use language with accuracy, clarity, and discrimination, to interpret data, to appraise evidence and evaluate arguments, to recognize the existence (or non-existence) of logical relationships between propositions, to draw warranted conclusions and generalizations, to put to test the conclusions and generalizations at which one arrives, to reconstruct one's patterns of beliefs on the basis of wider experience, and to render accurate judgments about specific things and qualities in everyday life.

Critical thinking can occur whenever one judges, decides, or solves a problem; in general, whenever one must figure out what to believe or what to do, and do so in a reasonable and reflective way. Reading, writing, speaking, and listening can all be done critically or uncritically. Critical thinking is crucial to becoming a close reader and a substantive writer. Expressed most generally, critical thinking is 'a way of taking up the problems of life.' Irrespective of the sphere of thought, 'a well-cultivated critical thinker':

- raises important questions and problems, formulating them clearly and precisely;
- gathers and assesses relevant information, using abstract ideas to interpret it effectively;

- comes to well-reasoned conclusions and solutions, testing them against relevant criteria and standards;
- thinks open-mindedly within alternative systems of thought, recognizing and assessing, as need be, their assumptions, implications, and practical consequences; and
- communicates effectively with others in figuring out solutions to complex problems; without being unduly influenced by others' thinking on the topic.

When individuals possess intellectual skills alone, without the intellectual traits of mind, *weak sense critical thinking* results. Fair-minded or *strong sense critical thinking* requires intellectual humility, empathy, integrity, perseverance, courage, autonomy, confidence in reason, and other intellectual traits. Thus, critical thinking without essential intellectual traits often results in clever, but manipulative and often unethical or subjective thought.

"And what a fine way to describe how the intellectuals in your modern society think: 'clever, but manipulative and often unethical,'" says Narayan.

"Whereas your masses simply don't think at all," adds Scogan.

"Unthinking and cretinous at middle and base, cleverly insane at the tiptop. It's no wonder," Narayan continues, "because you don't teach your people actually *how to* think. But here in Pala, from Day One of kindergarten through the highest levels of university, we teach critical thinking skills and foster the qualities necessary for them: intellectual humility, empathy, integrity, perseverance, courage, autonomy, confidence in reason."

"Forgive me. But this whole chapter is you boasting about how your shit doesn't smell which is really nothing to boast about since the most delectable feces are always the shittiest smelling according to any accredited coprophagia connoisseur,"

I bark, considering the turd I just dropped in the hallway. "So intellectual humility doesn't stand out as one of your prominent traits."

"I don't think that's true," says Narayan. "We realize we don't know everything. In fact, we understand that as mortal humans our views will always be incomplete. It's beyond any human's capabilities to possess a God's-eye view."

"And it will always be this way—part of the human condition—that our knowledge will forever be limited and imperfect," proffers Moses. "*If* life has any meaning, the human mind will *always* be far too limited to grasp it. And if life will never fully reveal itself to even the brightest humans, then really what is the difference between being 'wise' and being a fool?"

"I agree, up to a point. Which is the point, I suppose," says Narayan. "Life may always elude meaning for even the wisest. But one should still draw lines between what will likely improve the life we have and what will likely not.

"*Is* there a meaning to this existence? Carl Jung was transfixed by the idea that life was not a series of random events but rather an expression of a deeper order. This deeper order led to the insights that a person was both embedded in an orderly framework and was the focus of that orderly framework and that the realization of this was more than just an intellectual exercise but also having elements of a spiritual awakening.

"Or perhaps the imaginative genius of Jung was wrong. Maybe there is no deeper order. Maybe it's all chaotic meaninglessness. Perhaps nihilism is the closest thing we humans can come to describing the universal state of affairs, but even if that's true, so what? To what end nihilism? No. Better to choose a lie to live by. Because if nihilism is correct, they're *all lies* anyway! But do choose your lie well. Choose a *good* lie!"

Moses: "And what lie do you live by in Pala?"

Narayan: "That it is worthy to protect and defend life. *All life*. By protecting and defending planetary life, we protect and defend ourselves."

Moses: "You protect and defend the pathogens causing human disease?"

"TB is life!" I bark with tear in eye.

"We of course combat the microorganisms that cause human disease," says Narayan. "Disease is one of Nature's mechanisms for keeping populations under control and in balance with the environment. If we nullify this mechanism by treating disease, the onus is then on us to limit our population. So we heal our sick, and hence use birth control to keep us in balance with our surroundings. Protecting and defending all life means protecting and defending the natural balance of life."

Guano: "Oh! More of that humility shining through!"

Narayan: "I think showing deference to the planetary system of life is exhibiting great humility. We Palanese understand our place as humans in this world far better than your modern culture, which long ago traded humility for hubris.

"Intellectual humility is inherent in Palanese culture because, although we use and appreciate it, we understand the limitations of human logic. Your modern society actually puts the human mind above all else. And has since Plato. Fracturing the mind from body. Never admitting that logic is just a tool; and like any tool, it has its uses and has its limitations.

"We use logic to hopefully help us make better decisions; to help us live better lives in the here and now; to help plan and protect our future. That's all logic is good for. We never glorify logic to the detriment of the more corporeal qualities necessary to make a whole, integrated human being. Your culture, in the forms of science and technology, *worships* logic, which has paradoxically led you to lives that are inherently illogical.

"Acknowledging the chasmal differences between our cultures is not boasting. Comparing ourselves favorably to you is simply pointing out how unwell you are. It's not boasting; it's recognizing the facts of the situation which are plain for anyone with eyes to see. But it doesn't have to be this way for you."

Narayan opens the door to another classroom. Inside, boys and girls similar in age to the previous class sit at desks reading Aldous Huxley's *Island.*

"Aesthetically, *Island* was Aldous Huxley's poorest written novel. It lacks the cutting wit and nimbleness of language typical of Huxley's writing. And still, still, *Island* is absolutely indispensable reading. It is nothing short of a blueprint for a good society," says Scogan.

Guano: "The ideas we've broached in this chapter are in Huxley's *Island*, along with many other pertinent concepts. I grant you Huxley's passage on how x-raying a child's wrist can reveal psychological development problems is laughable nonsense. And the moksha-medicine is a utopian panacea not equal to the very real solutions presented in the book (the moksha-medicine being a way for Huxley to encourage people to explore altered states of consciousness). Ho ho! And your cold intellectual cynics will have much fun at the expense of the yoga of love! Far be it from cold intellectual cynics to be able to imagine a life where being in tune with one's physical nature can lead to psychological and spiritual equanimity. No no! They've retreated too far into their own narrow intellects to allow for that! In any event, for the few dated or peculiar ideas in *Island* there are scores more of enlightened observations on how to build a sustainable, decent society of self-actualized human beings. It's a book as relevant today as it was fifty years ago."

Narayan: "*Island* may not be a masterpiece if all one is interested in is belles-lettres (see the modern mainstream reader), but if one is ready for literature that constructively instructs, that challenges, that leads to growth and wisdom, then *Island* is essential. It's the book we start all our pupils out on."

It doesn't have to be this way. Humanity can be better. Read

Island.

Scogan: "Read *Brave New World Revisited.* Read *Point Counter Point.* Read *all* of Huxley's novels and essays."

"You venerate Aldous Huxley here," Moses confirms more than asks.

"Oh, Huxley is well venerated in Pala," responds Narayan. "A first-rate intellectual who never let his powerful mind limit his extraordinary powers of perception. He was a true visionary. How ironic for a man with such foresight to be almost blind! A great thinker and seer—the most important writer of the twentieth century. Your culture would do well to rediscover him. And heed him."

A tall man with gray hair approaches Scogan and whispers something into his ear. "Ah, yes. Thank you, Mr. Rao. I'll be right there." The man nods, walks back down the hallway and exits the school. Scogan turns to Moses and me. "My assistant Mr. Rao tells me one of our vital projects requires my presence. I think this particular project would be of great interest to you. You are welcome to accompany me, if you'd like."

"Smells like teen spirit. We accept," I bark.

Outside the school, a group of teenagers with mountaineering gear is assembling. "Your Crips and Bloods are underarmed here. It's nearly impossible to execute a credible drive-by using a tent pole. I have tried," I bark.

Narayan says: "Some of our older students are setting off for a weeklong backpacking trip. Physical exertion is as important as mental exercise. One can't have a truly sound mind without a sound body. And just as critical thinking is a lifelong endeavor, so too is working one's body. Physicality puts us in touch with the here and now—our momentary existence. It prevents the tendency for humans to hide in the intellect, to the detriment of the whole human being." She laughs and shakes her head. "Your modern intellectuals are all sitting-addicts. That's why most of you are so repulsively unwholesome."

An old jeep pulls up to the front of the school. "Our ride," says Scogan, opening the door for me and Moses. We climb into the backseat, Scogan in front with Mr. Rao driving. "I'm sorry your introduction to the basics of Palanese education had to be so brief," says Mrs. Narayan at the side of our car. "I hope we've made a good impression on you."

"A good impression, yes," Moses tells her. "And a lasting one."

"Like a fine welt," I bark.

We exchange goodbyes and drive off, Narayan waiving from the front of the school. The jeep winds its way through the town and is soon rising above it, gripping the dirt of a small road zig-zagging up a mountain slope. The narrow path climbs steeply, a tenuous passage through the dense jungle closed around us. From the front seat Scogan turns to address us, speaking loudly so as to be heard over the whine of the jeep's engine and the cacophony of sounds calling and screeching from the luxuriant tangle surrounding us. "It's a pity you didn't see the gifted classes at school," he says.

"Gifted classes?" asks Moses.

"Special classes for our most gifted students. Classes designed especially to cultivate their unique creativity. Oh, we naturally seek to stoke the imaginations of all our citizens. But the specially gifted ones deserve special attention," responds Scogan. He pauses briefly, then continues: "Humans will always be divided into the categories of ordinary and extraordinary. With the extraordinary comprising a very, very small minority. Zeroes and ones, if you will. A good society allows the ordinary people equal opportunities and the right to have a meaningful say in their own lives: to live in freedom.

"By 'freedom' I mean the opportunity to empower themselves by pursuing real goals, not the artificial goals so readily manufactured by your society, and without interference, manipulation, or supervision from any large organization.

Freedom means being in control (either as an individual or as a member of a *small* group) of the life-and-death issues of one's existence; food, clothing, shelter, and defense against whatever threats there may be in one's environment. Freedom means having power; not the power to control other people but the power to control the circumstances of one's own life."

Guano: "Real freedom! Just like in the land of the free, America! Where Americans are all free to access their local community's natural resources which are not owned and controlled by corporate or government powers!"

Scogan: "One does not have freedom if anyone else (especially a large organization) has power over one, no matter how benevolently, tolerantly, and permissively that power may be exercised. It is important not to confuse freedom with mere permissiveness.

"Your modern society is in certain respects extremely permissive. In matters that are irrelevant to the functioning of the system you can generally do what you please. You can believe in any religion you like (as long as it does not encourage behavior that is dangerous to the system). You can go to bed with anyone you like. You can do anything you like as long as it is *unimportant*. But in all *important* matters the system tends increasingly to regulate your behavior.

"So, as stated, a good society allows the ordinary people equal opportunities and the right to have control over the decisions affecting their lives. But it also means the *extraordinary* people are afforded special privileges that come with extraordinary talent."

"Like the extraordinary talent to lick one's own cock," I bark, demonstrating in the backseat.

Moses says to Scogan, "So you devote additional resources to your most gifted children in order to develop their creative powers for the good of your society."

"For the good of individualism! Individualism in its

many forms!" Scogan gives a crooked smile and continues: "Eccentricity...It's the justification of all aristocracies. It justifies leisured classes and inherited wealth and privilege and endowments and all the other injustices of that sort. If you're to do anything reasonable in this world, you must have a class of people who are secure, safe from public opinion, safe from poverty, leisured, not compelled to waste their time in the imbecile routines that go by the name of Honest Work. You must have a class of which the members can think and, within the obvious limits, do what they please. You must have a class in which people who have eccentricities can indulge them and in which eccentricity in general will be tolerated and understood. That's the important thing about an aristocracy. Not only is it eccentric itself—often grandiosely so; it also tolerates and even encourages eccentricity in others. The eccentricities of the artist and the new-fangled thinker don't inspire it with that fear, loathing, and disgust which the burgesses instinctively feel towards them. It is a sort of Red Indian Reservation planted in the midst of a vast horde of Poor Whites—colonials at that. Within its boundaries wild men disport themselves—often, it must be admitted, a little grossly, a little too flamboyantly; and when kindred spirits are born outside the pale it offers them some sort of refuge from the hatred which the Poor Whites, *en bons bourgeois*, lavish on anything that is wild or out of the ordinary. Your modern society, in its base hunger for efficiency and commercial success, has little room for Reservations; the Redskins have been drowned in the great sea of Poor Whites.

"Pala is many things, among them: the last refuge for Red Indians!

"Your modern society is keen on telling itself that it is highly individualistic. The type of clothes you wear, your hairstyle, your grooming habits, the tattoos you sport, the music you listen to, the TV shows you watch, the car you drive, what you consume in general, your passion for making public the minutiae and inanities of your personal life through social media, your homogenized beliefs packaged to look meretriciously dissimilar, the novelty of the names you give to your children—your experts through your media explain to you that through these ways and others your society shows its individualistic nature. Of course in reality it's all superficial and vain. You *are* narcissistic, a far cry from individualistic. How you moderns actually live is comically similar. How the vast majority of you moderns think is methodically uniform. Modern mass society creates mass-men. Mass-men who love to be told how individualistic they are, how free they are, et cetera."

"So it's good to be one of the eccentric extraordinary ones here," I bark. "But what about your dullards?"

Scogan: "We keep our population in check, so there is plenty for all. And our economic system ensures a far more equitable distribution of resources. Consequently it's no wonder how much more aware and better adapted even our least talented citizens are compared to a drone with comparable abilities in your modern world."

From the driver's seat, Mr. Rao remarks: "I am not a bright man. I am secure enough to admit it. But although I may be slow, I know the answer to this question: Is it better to be an intelligent man in an insane society or a stupid man in a good society?"

We drive for at least a couple of hours, seeing no signs of mankind besides the narrow road carved into the jungle, before finally reaching a mountaintop cleared of enough vegetation for a small observatory. Moses offers: "A natural landscape unspoiled as far as the eye can see. Come nightfall, I'm sure the stars are an inspiring sight up here."

"The stars at night are big and bright, deep in the heart of Pala!" replies Scogan.

We enter the observatory through a door at its base. Inside, a half-dozen scientists busily pore over their computers and machinery. “Welcome!” a gravelly voice calls from above. It belongs to some old motherfucker smiling down at us from a raised metal platform, I bark! The man descends a spiral staircase and walks to us. Below a crop of chaotic silver hair is a face, heavily lined, yet vital. Swimming in the whites of his eyes are large probing pupils, salient black orbs ringed with thin circles of steel blue. Eyes that despite their age suggest uncommon lucidity and sharpness. “Welcome! You must be our guests from abroad,” he greets. “I am Rogue Rotkilt.”

“Rogue Rotkilt!” Moses and I ejaculate in unison. We wipe. We ask: “*The* Rogue Rotkilt?”

“I can see my reputation still precedes me. I should think I would have been forgotten by now.”

Rogue Rotkilt. Multibillionaire. Literally lost to history when forty years ago he vanished. “Or dropped out,” Rotkilt says. “To help build *this*.”

“Among his many, many accomplishments, Mr. Rotkilt founded Pala,” says Scogan.

“Not I alone!” laughs Rotkilt. “I had the help of many intelligent, decent people.”

“Humility aside, Pala would never have been if not for the man standing before you,” Scogan compliments. “The building of Pala was his idea. Even more important: Pala was financed by him.”

“Financing, you say? What do the interest rates look like for a floating Love Canal?” I bark.

“You should know by now we don’t believe in charging interest here in Pala,” Rotkilt answers with a wink.

Scogan says: “In order for life to take hold on the garbage, natural topsoil had to be brought here decades ago. It was a humungous project requiring the excavation of countless billions of tons of soil which then had to be transported to freighters for shipping. All done in secret. Without the wealth and power of one of the modern world’s most prominent oligarchs, it could have never been accomplished."

Rotkilt: "So I dropped out of sight those many years ago. Presumed dead by everyone but the most comical conspiracy theorists."

"*Conspiracy?* For the sake of a *New York Times* bestseller I'll have to start listening to this old motherfucker," I bark!

Rotkilt: "I did not relinquish control of my empire; the reins were always firmly in my hands, clandestinely. Rotkilt Industries—a cornerstone of what I had come to understand was a system destined to enslave or destroy humanity—would now build a society that could save humanity.

"I thought creating a sane, good society would teach the rest of the world that it didn't have to be this way. That there were real alternatives. But I was wrong in that. In the country of the insane, the integrated man doesn't get welcomed. He gets lynched.

"The modern masses don't want to be saved. They just want to continue to gorge and tranquilize themselves. You know, the anarchists are the best of your lot. They are the noble idealists. But they are also the naïvest of fools. They keep waiting on the people to throw off their shackles and free themselves. Of course the people never do. And the anarchists can never figure it out. They can't—or won't—grasp that the masses will not free themselves because they are simply not as *good* as the anarchists are. In fact, the average man is as cowardly and base as he has ever been. And *greedier* than ever thanks to a system that cultivates such traits in order to make better consumers and passive subjects.

"I finally realized: In the world of the insane, the integrated country doesn't get welcomed. It gets assimilated or annihilated. By military aggression or slower absorption into your imperious Mother Culture, Pala inevitably will perish. Assimilated or annihilated. It's what your culture does. And has for thousands of years."

He pauses and lets out a small sigh. "The only reason Pala has survived this long is because we're an isolated island. We've been able to elude your detection and grow something different, something better. There is no way Pala would have been able to germinate in your midst. We would have been perceived as a threat to you. And we *are* a threat to you. Because you are a threat to us, and all life on the Earth."

Lightly tapping his fingers together in thought, Rotkilt concludes: "There needs to be a pause. Mankind needs to pause to reflect on who he is and who he wants to be. At this time in history, there needs to be a pause in technological progress to allow man to find himself, and to *evolve*. There needs to be more Palas."

Moses: "And yet there can be no more Palas because, as you say, our Mother Culture will kill them."

Rotkilt: "Unless someone stops you. Unless someone *kills* your Mother Culture."

Moses: "And how is that possible? As you say, the masses just want to gorge and tranquilize themselves. They're far too lazy and pusillanimous to even look in the mirror, let alone *change* themselves."

Aldous Huxley: "If human beings were shown what they're really like, they'd either kill one another as vermin, or hang themselves."

"It's true," nods Rotkilt. "Your modern society creates emotional cripples, psychologically stunted children in adult bodies. Inflexible, intractable. Incapable of self-directed reflection and change. You authentically need large authoritarian social structures to keep the brats in line. So, if the children will not take the medicine they need of their own volition, they'll be force-fed it.

"Humanity is wilting because of overcentralization. And yet the centralization of power is demanded by your powers that be because, one: a complex technological society *must* be highly organized (centralized) to function most efficiently; and two: the broken, irresponsible people it creates must be supervised, as discussed. What it amounts to is this: At this point in history, humanity desperately needs a reversal of this process of centralization—humanity needs *decentralization*; but humanity hasn't been raised to be responsible enough for the freedoms of a decentralized society (i.e., a Palanese society). So, paradoxically, the only way to reverse the disastrous course of overcentralization is with even more short-term centralization.

"If the masses of modern society are incapable of changing themselves and their society, if change cannot happen from the bottom up, then change must be instituted from the top down. If the children will not take the medicine they need of their own volition, they'll be force-fed it through their own large authoritarian institutions. That was the thought a year ago when I formed the Malthusian League of the Rogue."

Rotkilt smiles to himself, then continues: "The Malthusian League of the Rogue. Having determined that the people of the modern world were incapable of seeing Pala as a constructive lesson, I decided to reveal our presence to only a few select individuals. Individuals possessing open eyes with the necessary self-confidence and quickness of mind to allow them to use their own eyes. Individuals who were also extraordinarily wealthy and influential.

"These few individuals were invited to Pala. And they saw for themselves what humanity could be if its potential were actually tapped. They were already aware of the problems humanity presented to itself and the natural world. Now they saw the solution. Together we formed the League. A conspiracy of enlightened oligarchs."

"A conspiracy? God bless you, sir! We're assured of a best-seller via the modern mainstream dullard demographic. Now if you include the Knights Templar in the conspiracy I will lick your asshole," I bark as I lick my asshole.

Rotkilt: "If modern society would not change from the bottom up, the men and women of the League would change it from the top down. If Palanese Culture could not take root elsewhere in the world because of your Mother Culture, then your Mother Culture would be uprooted.

"The League's objectives were, one: eliminate the threat of nuclear holocaust by eliminating all nuclear weapons worldwide; two: free the minds of the younger generations by teaching children critical thinking skills through all levels in all schools, coupled with an educative dose of ecology; three: begin to reverse catastrophic human overpopulation by instituting worldwide policies that reward couples for having no children or one child, and having that one child later in their lives; four: dismember the highly centralized economic system of global capitalism (the engine driving runaway technology, the machine breeding greedy shortsighted automatons) and replace it with decentralized, local economies which redefine property along use-and-occupancy lines and prohibit usury (interest and rent)."

Moses: "You are talking a full-scale revolution. You are talking blasting the very foundation of modern society and completely replacing it. How could you possibly succeed in this?"

Rotkilt: "The power of a handful of the richest people on the planet should not be underestimated. Capitalism has allowed for a deleterious concentration of wealth in only a few hands. A cabal of multibillionaires has access to incredible resources when one considers that 1 percent of the planet's population owns 40 percent of the entire planet's wealth. Indeed, your system has always been a tool for the wealthy. Consent from the masses is so easily manufactured in your so-called democracies that they're hardly democracies at all. They're *plutocracies.* They're *oligarchies* based on keeping wealth and power in the limited hands that already have wealth and power. Only now we would change that to an *enlightened* oligarchy—a new noble aristocracy not based on heredity, but based on wisdom, that would radically change the direction of humanity so that future humans could be trusted with *real* democracy.

"With our objectives set, my colleagues and I used the immense wealth at our disposal to put a plan to action. Behind closed doors, we began applying pressure to the U.S. president to lead on nuclear disarmament. Not the same disingenuous lip service certain 'progressive' presidents have paid to nuclear disarmament in the past. *Real* disarmament.

"America is the only country powerful enough to impress upon the rest of the world that nuclear weapons are the enemy of all life. If the unacceptable threat of nuclear weapons is to ever be extinguished, if the presence of nuclear weapons is to ever be called what it really is—the worst of all crimes—then America must lead the way. America, the superpower, is the only country with the power to compel *all* nations of the world to dispel the omnicidal anathema of nuclear weapons.

"So, through enticements, bribery, and threats of a political and more corporeal nature, we would impress upon the president of the United States, and later Congress during the ratification phase, that nuclear weapons must be abandoned in order to increase humanity's long-term chances of survival. The president would in turn entice/coerce Russia and the other minor nuclear powers to disarm under the framework of the United Nations (U.N. weapons inspectors to verify full-disarmament compliance from *all* nations). With the threat of planetary nuclear annihilation finally expunged, the League would devote the full of our resources to our other objectives.

"Where public and private schools could be worked with, critical thinking skills and ecology would be taught. When educational institutions resisted us, the League would set up its own private schools, hiring the best teachers away from those neighboring schools bent on destructive recalcitrance.

"When we could, the League would work with local, state, and federal governments, along with international organizations, to ensure universal access to all methods of family planning. When governments could not be relied upon, we'd set up and fund private centers offering free birth control, abortions, and other fertility-control services. We would encourage governments to reverse disastrous tax codes that reward the populace for having children when obviously the diametric opposite is needed. We began to initiate a worldwide program that would pay women of childbearing age a monthly stipend *not* to have children."

"How does that work?" asks Moses.

"It's quite simple," answers Rotkilt. "Any woman between, say, the ages of fifteen and thirty-five, goes to one of the League's clinics where they are administered a pregnancy test. If the result of the test is negative, they receive money. They can return every month for another test and money. If they become pregnant, they do not receive funds. A potent weapon against overpopulation, the results promised to be extraordinary.

"In the arena of economics, the League would issue no-interest loans to start thousands of worker-owned-and-controlled businesses. We developed plans for our own small communities with property rights based on use and occupancy. We encouraged local governments to pass laws making property ownership contingent on use and occupancy. However, very, very few governments would work with us on this front since it was an overt declaration of war against the vested interests that control governments. We should have waited on this. It was too soon. Although I suppose it's irrelevant *when* we tried to implement economic revolution. Because the League was doomed to failure from the start."

"Doomed from the start?" asks Moses. "You mean none of this worked?"

I bark at Moses: "Dear dope, it didn't work because:

A. Modern humans are far too reasonable to remove the nuclear revolver from their temple.
B. When children start coming home and questioning their modern parents' ever-reasonable beliefs using critical thinking skills learned in school then modern parents rejoice in having such wise, free-thinking children by burning down the enlightened children's school.
C. Any person insane enough to try to get between the modern cretins and their 'right' to breed cancerously will be personally burned down after school.
D. The hordes of modern cretins will not stand for overturning the system that enslaves them. The elite modern crazies will not stand for overturning the system that has made them rich and powerful."

"The League failed soon after it formed," laments Rotkilt. "As mentioned, in order to reverse centralization, even more short-term centralization is needed. The League needed a centralized world authority with the power to enforce the policies that would lead to decentralization (nuclear disarmament; education that develops and frees the mind instead of enslaving it; fair, local, and sustainable economics; a human population in balance with the natural world), and we needed a centralized world authority with the power to police the billions of automatons to ensure they don't tear each other apart as the cultural institutions responsible for their programming are dismantled. We needed a world authority with the power to make the children take the medicine that would save them, despite themselves. But we failed to harness such a power. Ironically, your pseudo-democracy stands in the way of real future democracy because your citizenry is too scared of fundamental change, and will not have it.

"Your system has a mind of its own; a criminally insane mind, but a mind nonetheless. When our initiatives started recently coming to light, the system needed little effort to manufacture consent from the masses to oppose the revolution. Your Mother Culture through her mass media whores labeled us malcontents and misanthropes, mere laughingstocks. But when some of our beleaguered programs still showed signs that they may yet be effective and become a genuine danger to the system, we were upgraded to madmen, enemies of the state, and of course, terrorists.

"So be it.

"The brave members of the League who put their own fortunes on the line now find their lives at risk as well. We are being hunted. The latest monsters of the week to justify First World—primarily American—military aggression which justifies the trillions of dollars spent on military technology which justifies the military-industrial-technological base of your malefic economic system. But the League's attempts to breathe life into a better humanity will not go in vain." Rotkilt winks. "Luckily, I have a Plan B."

"Thank God this is finally going somewhere. For the sake of mainstream reading dullards and *New York Times* bestselling steaming piles, bring on the mainstream trivialities posing as important topics and celebrities and whores," I bark.

"Rotkilt Industries has developed several technologies which, unlike most modern technologies, will serve to break mankind's self-imposed enslavement." Rotkilt points his finger towards a large monitor hanging on the observatory wall. "That video screen shows one such technology being utilized in Plan B, which is short for Plan Bollocks.

"What you are seeing is a satellite view of a stretch of Interstate 15 running through the Mojave Desert. We have all two-hundred-plus miles of I-15 between Los Angeles and Las Vegas under the supervision of dozens of Rotkilt Industries satellites in geostationary orbit over the highway. What you do not see is the radiation beaming from those satellites onto all two-hundred-plus miles of I-15 between L.A. and Las Vegas."

"Now that's what I call a *glowing* reference!" I bark!

Rotkilt: "Anyone who chooses to live in Los Angeles should not be breeding. Anyone who chooses to visit Las Vegas should not be breeding. Now, thanks to irradiating satellites, the millions of cretins visiting Las Vegas from Los Angeles *will not* be breeding."

"I'd give that a *glowing* review!" Moses barks.

"Also being irradiated: anyone choosing to watch a Sandra Bullock movie and of course NASCAR fans," promises Rotkilt. "Unfortunately with a distended population of seven billion, the halfwits are reproducing faster than we can sterilize them. We need something more. It's late in the game and we need a home run." Rotkilt motions us to follow him up the spiral staircase to a metal platform. At the top he pulls a sheet from a massive cylindrical object revealing:

The Big Gay Gun

"The Big Gay Gun!" Rotkilt announces. "The crown jewel in Plan Bollocks."

"And perhaps: the *family jewel!*"

"Ha!"

"Ha!"

"Ha!"

"Ha!"

"The Big Gay Gun. Harnessing big gay technology, it fires a big gay ray that will turn an area the size of Texas gay." Rotkilt cocks the underside of the Big Gay Gun's shaft, prompting the weapon's dangling 'n pierced power sack to contract. An awesome! gay wad shoots out of the Gun's tip towards the horizon, in the general direction of Texas.

Rotkilt: "With Texas now one hundred percent gay, the males there will be busy buggering each other even more than usual. Between taking in musicals and anal fisting, they'll have no time to reproduce. In fact the thought of vagina will lead to mass nausea and panic and shopping. Over the next decades, their dwindling numbers will be content to mindlessly consume with a special emphasis placed on pop culture inanities. That is: leading the typical American life. *But without the breeding!* After they and their culture have finally withered away, Texas will be ready for a new culture from a new people whose modest ambition is to live as fully human beings in harmony with the rest of the life in Texas and on this planet."

"Make Texas a utopia? You *are* madmen!" I bark.

"If only that were true. Because everything that ever gets done in this world is done by madmen," suggests Scogan. "We sane men have never achieved anything. We're too sane; merely reasonable. We lack the human touch, the compelling enthusiastic mania. People are quite ready to listen to the philosophers for a little amusement, just as they would listen to a fiddler or a mountebank. But as to acting on the advice of the men of reason—never. Wherever the choice has had to be made between the man of reason and the madman, the world has unhesitatingly followed the madman. For the madman appeals to what is fundamental, to passion and the instincts; the philosophers to what is superficial and supererogatory—reason.

"Consider, for example, the case of Luther and Erasmus." Scogan takes out a pipe and begins to fill it as he talks. "There was Erasmus, a man of reason if ever there was one. People listened to him at first—a new virtuoso performing on that elegant and resourceful instrument, the intellect; they even admired and venerated him. But did he move them to behave as he wanted them to behave—reasonably, decently, or at least a little less porkishly than usual? He did not. And then Luther appears, violent, passionate, a madman insanely convinced about matters in which there can be no conviction. He shouted, and men rushed to follow him. Erasmus was no longer listened to; he was reviled for his reasonableness. Luther was serious, Luther was reality—like the great modern wars. Erasmus was only reason and decency; he lacked the power, being a sage, to move men to action. Europe followed Luther and embarked on a century and a half of war and bloody persecution. It's a melancholy story." Scogan lights a match. In the intense light the flame is all but invisible. The smell of burning tobacco warmly overpowers the sterilized air of the observatory.

"If you want to get men to act reasonably, you must set about persuading them in a maniacal manner. The very sane precepts of the founders of religions are only made infectious by means of enthusiasms which to a sane man must appear deplorable. It is humiliating to find how impotent unadulterated sanity is. Sanity, for example, informs us that the only way in which we can preserve civilization is by behaving decently and intelligently. Sanity appeals and argues; your rulers persevere in their customary porkishness, while your masses acquiesce and obey. The only hope is a maniacal crusade. Are you, the reader of this book, ready to begin one? Being a person of intelligence and reason, you may feel a little ashamed partaking. However"—Scogan shrugs his shoulders and, pipe in hand, makes a gesture of resignation—"it's futile to complain that things are as they are. The fact remains that sanity unassisted is useless. What we want, then, is a sane and reasonable exploitation of the forces of insanity. And sane men will have the power yet." Scogan's eyes shine with a more than ordinary brightness.

"Yes," he continues, "the time has come. We men of intelligence must harness the insanities to the service of reason. We can't leave the world any longer to the direction of chance. We can't allow dangerous maniacs like Luther, mad about dogma, like Napoleon, mad about himself, to go on casually appearing and turning everything upside down; or worse, keeping things as they are. In the past it didn't so much matter; but our modern machine is too powerful. Another knock like even a smallish regional nuclear war, another Luther or two, and the whole concern will go to pieces. The time has come for the men of reason to canalize the madness of the world's maniacs into proper channels, to make it do useful work, like a mountain torrent driving a dynamo..."

"Making electricity to light a Swiss hotel," I bark. "You ought to complete the simile."

Scogan waves away the interruption. "There's only one thing to be done," he says. "The men of intelligence must combine, must conspire, and seize power from the imbeciles and maniacs who now direct the world. Will the reader of this book join us?"

Rotkilt: "*Or*, you could build yourself a Big Gay Gun and turn the mad world into fruitless fruits; ensuring they all eventually *peter* out!"

"Ha!"

"Ha!"

"Ha!"

"Ha!"

Rotkilt: "Texas is only the beginning. The Big Gay Gun has the rest of the modern world in its sights!"

Editor's note: The Big Gay Gun experiences a refractory

period immediately following a discharge, during which time the Big Gay Gun is unable to achieve another ejection but also feels a deep and often pleasurable sense of relaxation. The duration of the refractory period varies considerably. Age affects the recovery time, with younger Big Gay Guns typically recovering faster than older Big Gay Guns, though not universally so.

Rotkilt: "Allowing for a good couple hours' rest between firings, I figure it'll take the Big Gay Gun four days to shoot a load all over America; a couple weeks to slather Japan, Europe, and the other remaining centers of your Mother Culture; a couple months for the Third World leftovers."

Editor's note: Then we just wait for them to sodomize and lisp their way out of existence.

"Not a bad gig if you can get it," lisps Moses.

This is my pity for all that is past: I see how all of it is abandoned—abandoned to the pleasure, the spirit, the madness of every generation, which comes along and reinterprets all that has been as a bridge to itself.

A great despot might come along, a shrewd monster who, according to his pleasure and displeasure, might constrain and strain all that is past till it becomes a bridge to him, a harbinger and herald and cockcrow.

This, however, is the other danger and what prompts my further pity: whoever is of the rabble, thinks back as far as the grandfather; with the grandfather, however, time ends.

Thus all that is past is abandoned: for one day the rabble might become master and drown all time in shallow waters.

Therefore, my brothers, a NEW NOBILITY is needed, which shall be the adversary of all rabble and of all that is despotic, and shall inscribe anew the word "noble" on new tables.

For many noble ones are needed, and many kinds of noble ones, FOR A NEW NOBILITY! Or, as I once said in parable: "That is just divinity, that there are Gods, but no God!"

Thus spake Zarathustra.

"For a new nobility with noble new tables to rise, ignobility must fall!" Rotkilt cries, firing the Big Gay Gun at, say, Southern California. In the afterglow we enjoy a deep and pleasurable sense of relaxation. We light cigarettes. Rotkilt picks up the regal Maine Coon cat from offstage. The old man delivers his line: "Cat curled up in sinister mastermind's arms. Popular fiction cliché of supervillain representing the stock character of the evil genius."

"Thank God. There's no other way we're going to get ourselves an *NYT* bestseller," I bark.

"Hmph! Le chien est très stupide! Mais il est exact," dit le chat.

My dangling afterglow and cigarette are ruined by the explosion on the observatory floor. Hellevator bursts up through the ground, opens its doors, and shoots out a wad of fireball and forked tongue and: *Oat Man!*

Hellevator: "*Ding!*"

Guano: "Hello, Third World dreg. I thought you were busy in the can being orificially manslaughtered. In the can."

Oat Man: "Oh yes, sir. Quite busy with that. In prison I joined a gang by orificially accepting the gang. All at once. Every day. That prison gang was: *the Knights Templar!*"

"Calling all literary agents whoring themselves out (orificially) to corporate executive pimps!" I bark!

Oat Man: "The head of the Knights Templar is Hellevator. While I gave the head head on date night, Hellevator turned the proverbial tables and fork tongued and swallowed me, spitting me out here, sir."

Guano: "*A Third World dreg being sexually victimized by the Knights Templar who are secretly led by a First World Hellevator.* For you modern reading dullards scoring at home, that's:

- Mainstream trivialities posing as important topics.
- Conspiracies.
- Whores.

- A celebrity wholly untalented and whorely gifted to play me in the movie version. Like Sandra Bullock."

My dangling afterglow is ruined by the explosion through the observatory roof. Bursting through hole and shooting his wad of parachute is: *Texas Justice!*

"Not even the dullest of modern reading dullards could miss this coming!" I bark!

Also crashing through domed roof: Lucky Lonestar, Red Hardtongue, Hoss Bullchatter, Thick Bullard. "Time for a little *Texas Justice!*" they hoot and slap each other's asses and vas deferens.

(Plural: vasa deferentia.)

"From Texas, you say? Well, at least we know the Big Gay Gun works," says Rotkilt.

"Nah. They've always been this flamboyantly heroic," I bark as Rotkilt's afterglow is ruined by the explosions from Pala being carpet bombed. "But don't worry. Through military annihilation and cultural assimilation, Pala will be transformed into the garbage pile it was meant to be."

CUT TO:

EXT. PALA — SUNSET

The day is coming to an end in PARADISE. A light breeze blows through FIELDS OF GOLD. The theme music is Sting's "Fields of Gold," the song's rights having been acquired by our particular supranational corporate steaming pile along with Sting's marvelous genitals. There, in PARADISE, a HELICOPTER SHOT sweeps to the end of FIELDS OF GOLD where BULLDOZERS are CLEARING the remaining natural FLORA and FAUNA in order to build The Man!santo's genetically modified FIELDS OF GOLD INDUSTRIAL AGRIBUSINESS FARMS COMPLEX, INC.

CUT TO:

In PARADISE, a HELICOPTER SHOT sweeps to the end of Pala's first FIELDS OF GOLD MAXIMUM SECURITY PRISON COMPLEX. The scene is serene and softly suspended. Inside PRISON inside PARADISE, a THIRD WORLD DREG in HALF AN ASS COSTUME who has always sought to LICK the ASSES of all nearby FIRST WORLD AUTHORITY FIGURES is LICKING the ASSES of all his cellmates who are: the KNIGHTS TEMPLAR!!!!!!!!!!!

which speeds straight out at the audience IN 3-D!

CUT TO:

In PARADISE, a HELICOPTER SHOT sweeps to the end of Pala's first FIELDS OF GOLD SUPER-REGIONAL SHOPPING MALL COMPLEX. HEROES sit at a TABLE outside the SHAKEY'S PIZZA inside the FOOD COURT inside PARADISE as Sting's "Fields of Gold" plays over the MALL SPEAKERS. The scene is serene and softly suspended:

"We did it all for a just cause, didn't we, Buck?" cries Lucky Lonestar.

Buck Masters wipes the tears from Lucky's swollen eyes and orifices. "Yeah, lil' buddy. We did it just 'cause."

"For freedom?" cries Lucky.

"For freedom," Buck consoles, crawling into Lucky's plastic chair, made in Third World shithole.

"For the children?" wails Lucky.

"For the children." They spoon.

"God bless you, Buck," chokes Lucky.

"God bless you, lil' fella."

"They draw close, looking into each other's eyes; slowly, steadily, erectly giving each other: two big thumbs-up!" Sandra Bullock barks!

CPSIA information can be obtained at www.ICGtesting.com
Printed in the USA
BVOW011539140911

271195BV00001B/10/P